A *William Joseph* Book

authorwilliamjoseph.weebly.com

Published by William Joseph 2019

CARNIVAL OF TERROR

Cover design by: Just Write Creations and Services
Formatting by: Dark Wish Designs

This book is dedicated to those who can find both laughter and strength in the darkest of times.

And to Greenlee Sage. May you grow up to become both as strong and fierce as some of the characters in this book.

"The clown may be the source of mirth, but who shall make the clown laugh?"
-Angela Carter

Part One

 # Chapter 1

"I love you so much," she whispered, her exhaling breath gently tickling my ear and sending a shudder through my body.

I rolled over and gazed into her big baby blue eyes, a smile creeping across my face as I mirrored her expression.

"I still can't believe that I get to wake up to you every morning for forever," I returned.

She smiled, this time a slight squeal of glee coming out as she raised her hand and stared at her wedding band.

I brought my hand up to hers, and we placed our palms together, staring at our matching rings for a brief second before kissing each other.

"I love you so much, Victor."

"I love you more my Isabella."

We kissed passionately for a few moments more before we both acknowledged that it was time to get up and begin our day. Our honeymoon wasn't going to last forever. We needed to get a jump on the day if we were going to enjoy ourselves. We already spent the first day of our honeymoon traveling to the Mid-West from home, and then spent the entire second day in bed. That was three days ago now. We promised each other that we would take the next few days and explore every avenue of fun that we could encounter, even if it meant complete exhaustion.

"Breakfast?" Isabella asked from the kitchen, wearing nothing but one of the soft white linen robes that came with our suite.

"The usual," I replied as I began to get dressed.

By the time I finished, there were two eggs over-easy on the plate with a few slices of bacon and two slices of toast.

"You're the best," I complimented, Isabella, smirking and then turning to plant a kiss on my lip as she adjusted my bow tie with a giggle.

"You're never going to figure these things out, are you?"

"Of course not. That's why I married you, silly."

"Oh, is that right?" she laughed, spinning the towel round and round as if she was going to whip me.

"Hey, play nice!" I shouted as I dodged several half swings.

"I'm a woman. We don't play fair," she winked and then let out a roar of a laugh.

I jumped in and kissed her before she could get off a full strike, distracting her long enough to sneakily grab a slice of toast off the plate on the table and then shove it in her mouth.

She bit into it with a growl, and we both broke out

into laughter because of it.

"So, what are we going to do today?" I inquired as I pulled out the chair and sat at the table.

"Hmm, let's see."

Isabella pranced around the kitchen with a newspaper that had been slid under our door while we slept.

"Some movies are playing at the local theater."

"I'd rather not spend it doing something we can just do at home."

She nodded and turned the page.

"There is a race track nearby that has some horse racing going on. Maybe we can place some bets and test that amazing luck of yours?" she said as she bumped her butt against me signaling that she wanted to sit on my lap.

I obliged.

"I'd rather not turn into your father this early into our marriage," I joked.

"Hey!" she responded, hitting me on the head with the paper. "That's not nice."

I laughed, and after a second, she did too as she opened the paper again and suddenly jumped up with a shout.

"I've got it!"

"What have you got?"

"There's a circus in town!" she informed in a high-pitched jubilant fashion.

I stared at her for a moment as she made her eyes big like a not-so-innocent little puppy would.

"Really, a circus?"

"Yes, look!"

She slammed the paper down on the table and pointed at the big black and white photo of the big striped tent with clowns standing out front.

"I don't know," I said knowing full well that she had made her mind up.

"Oh, c'mon Victor, it will be fun. When is the last time that you ever went to the circus?"

I thought about it for a moment, and she was right. I hadn't gone to a circus since I was a small kid. My parents had taken me, and I was so afraid of the clowns that my Dad had to carry me out before the main event even happened.

I sighed as I reluctantly nodded my head yes.

"Oh, thank you, thank you! This is going to be so much fun babe. You won't regret it. There's going to be so many things to do!"

She turned and kissed my cheek, throwing the paper up into the air as she danced her way into the other room and over to her clothes.

I couldn't help but smile as I stared down at my plate and continued to eat, saving one of the eggs and slices of bacon for her.

"I saved you some," I acknowledged as I passed her on the way to the bathroom.

She turned from her fully crouched position, knee-deep in clothes, and blew a kiss.

***

Once I was done applying gel to my hair, double-checking my shave was still clean, and I was done using the bathroom, I headed back out only to come to an immediate stop upon catching a glimpse of Isabella. There she stood beside the bed in an outfit that I had never seen her in before. She was wearing some black Mary-Jane heels, a yellow polka dot sundress, and already had her hair up in curls. She looked like she was straight out of a pin-up magazine.

"Hey handsome," she complimented, winking as she smacked her lips together to finish the application of her bright red lipstick.

I was speechless. Somehow, she was even more beautiful to me now than she ever had been before, and I thought just days ago her in her wedding dress had been the most beautiful time.

"Is everything okay baby?"

"Ye-yes," I replied, stuttering slightly and finding myself gravitating towards her as she turned to the mirror to continue to apply more makeup.

I walked up behind her and wrapped my arms around her tiny waist, resting my chin on her shoulder and looking our reflections in the eyes.

"We make one gorgeous couple, don't we?" she asked, as she gently tugged on the spiral of my mustache.

I was wearing brown oxfords, black pants, black

suspenders, a maroon shirt, a black vest, and my black bow tie. We didn't match much at all.

"You look a million times better than me. I should change."

"No," she said sternly, turning and placing her hand on my chest. "You look magnificent my love. After all, you complete my look. You're my best accessory."

I lowered my head and smirked as I ran my hand through my stiff hair feeling my face get warm and my cheeks turn rosy.

She giggled.

"You're never going to get used to me giving you compliments, are you?"

"One day, maybe," I replied as she lifted my chin with her finger.

"Well, I hope you never do. It's adorable when you blush, and I absolutely love that about you. It's quite precious."

She turned back to the mirror, our eyes still connected as she continued to do her makeup.

"What did I ever do to deserve you?"

"Hmm, I'm not so sure really," she responded with an expression of deep thought.

I laughed as I pinched her side and she let out a chuckle.

"I'll leave you be. Meet me outside when you're ready. I'll be waiting out front."

"Yes dear, try not to miss me too much while you're away," she joked.

***

I stood out front of the hotel enjoying my drag while I waited for Isabella to finish getting ready inside. The weather couldn't have been any better. The skies were bright and blue. There wasn't a cloud in sight, and the temperature was neither too warm nor too cold. Others passed by on the sidewalk with a smile or tip of the hat as cars rolled by, everyone going about their business. Everyone was so friendly here in Tennessee unlike back at home. New Yorkers were of a different breed I suppose.

"There you are!" Isabella's voice rang out, and I turned, catching a glimpse of her as she came out the front door, catching the attention of a man walking by with his wife and causing her to slap him on the arm.

"All ready to go?" I asked as she got closer, her bright blue eyes sparkling in the sunlight.

"Sure am! I've got the paper too. It has an address, but I'm not sure where that is."

"Oh, pardon me. Do you need some help?" an older lady passing by inquired as she came to a stop.

"Why yes, we do ma'am. We heard there was a circus in town, and we were thinking of checking it out."

"Oh," she said looking at us oddly for a brief second before turning to look up the street. "I forgot that that noisy bunch was in town. They come around every year. You can walk there if you'd like. It's just up this road here. Take a right turn, and it will be up on your left."

"Thank you so much," Isabella jumped in.

The older lady nodded her head and smiled before continuing back on her way.

"Let's go!" Isabella shouted in glee as her fingers slid in between mine and she clenched my hand.

 # Chapter 2

"It looks so much bigger in person!"

She was right, it did. The old lady's directions were spot on, and we arrived without issue.

Many people were flooding the streets as they approached the iron-wrought open gates and fence that seemed to surround the area. Out front were two tall men in suits, both with cigars in their mouths and a man at the podium between them yelling into a megaphone. We joined the crowd and flowed with them closer to the gates, paying the small entrance fee and making our way past the intimidating gate guards who towered over us. Once we were inside, the crowd spread out as families began to chase after kids who ran off in every direction while other couples stuck together and started to head off towards the big tent far off in the distance.

"This place is huge," Isabella said again as she pulled me forward towards a large yellow cart where someone was selling cotton candy.

I got the biggest one that he was selling and then handed it to Isabella, who wasted no time in ripping large chunks off and eating it.

"It's so good. Have a piece!"

I indulged.

"What do you want to do?" I asked with a laugh as she turned to me with a big smile, a piece of cotton candy hanging out of the side of her mouth.

"Is everything an option?"

***

We must have walked for hours as Isabella broke me from my slightly on-guard state of mind. I was so worried about seeing clowns that I hadn't even realized that we passed dozens of them. Being with her made me forget about all my other worries, and the clowns were not an issue, blending into the crowd as if just background noise. We rode on the Ferris wheel and a few other smaller rides before taking a lunch break. We then proceeded to go tent to tent and check out the freaks that were on display. There was a strong man, a dwarf dressed as if they were from a tribe, and a magician whose assistant never returned from disappearing. We played a few games, won a few small prizes, and a stuffed animal that Isabella gave to a little crying girl who accidentally let go of her balloon.

"What next?" I asked after, wondering if we were going to play some more games to try and win something again or if we were going to go on another ride.

"Want to check out the big tent now?"

"Sure," I replied as we then ran like a couple of high school kids who were madly in love towards the massive tent.

As we approached the big top, an elephant walked by, carrying a small child and his mother who were both sitting on top of it with the trainer standing fearlessly behind them. Once the animal passed, we darted forward again, entering the tent through the large opening we had seen others go through.

"Oh my god," Isabella said as she then let go of my hand and ran forward towards a bunch of cages.

I ran after and came to a stop just beside her as she peered into a large cage containing a bunch of baby tiger cubs wrestling with one another.

"How adorable!" she cried, covering her mouth with her hand.

We relished in the tiger cub's presence for a few minutes until Isabella moved onto a nearby pair of white horses standing tied to one of the big tent's massive poles. Other families had joined us as we continued to walk around and check out some of the other animals. There was a donkey, some hyenas, a bear, and a bunch of ducks behind a little mesh fence off to the side. After we were done looking at the animals, we continued through another opening in the side of the tent which opened and revealed the big interior. There were stands all around with many people already claiming seats for the big show, so we hurried and climbed up a few steps and got ourselves a spot. One of the weekly shows was about to begin, and I could not help but feed off Isabella's excitement as she clapped, her infectious smile spreading from cheek to cheek.

***

Everyone stood up and cheered as the man on the back of the elephant did a backflip onto a trampoline, went back up into the air and landed right back on top of the elephant again.

"That was amazing," I said as the show then concluded.

Isabella had her hands wrapped tightly around my arm as she closed her eyes and let out an exhausted sigh.

"Are you actually tired?" I said with a laugh.

"All of this excitement. It's so much in a single day. I'm pooped!" she replied while patting her belly.

"Hungry too?" I guessed, smirking as she looked up at me with her big blue eyes and batting her eyelashes at me.

I laughed.

"Okay, let's go get some food," I suggested as we then made our way out of the tent and then back out onto the concourse.

We moved with the rest of the exiting crowd but somehow got lost and found ourselves nowhere near where the food area was. Instead, we were by a bunch of trailers and were catching the eyes of some of the circus workers who didn't seem to be too pleased that we were there.

Isabella, while laughing hysterically, randomly began to run in between some of the trailers as I chased after her until she disappeared out of view. I shouted out to her several times, but there was no answer until I walked around a big brown tent and found her staring up at the front of it. Up on top of the tent were the large words "Fortune Teller," and as I came to a stop beside her, she turned and looked at me with a big smile inside.

"Wanna?" she asked.

"Sure, why not?"

We kissed before holding each other's hands and heading inside.

The interior was as dark and mysterious as one would expect a fortune teller's tent to be. As we continued in there was a doorway made of beads and seashells. We pushed through, revealing a large table at the center of a room with a large crystal ball on top and an older woman in a brown cloak sitting in a chair on the other side of the table.

"Come in, come in," she beckoned with a gap-filled smile.

Isabella sat down opposite the woman as I sat beside her.

"What would you like done today my dear?" the

fortune teller asked.

"Oh, I'm not so sure really. This is all so new to me. I have never been to a fortune-teller before."

"No worries my child," she replied with a grin as she waved her hands over her crystal ball. "I'll give you a simple reading for your first time, and free of charge."

"Oh, how wonderful! Thank you."

The fortune-teller smiled as she continued waving her hands over her ball, looking as if she was beginning to focus and then acting like she saw something. I did not really believe in fortune-telling or psychics. I always thought that they were a scam, but it was free, and Isabella really wanted to do it. I watched her face light up or react to every sound effect that the older lady made whenever she pretended to see something.

"I see a bright future ahead of you my child," the lady announced. "A life filled with love, a happy marriage, and a long life filled with laughter."

Isabella smiled.

"Ca-can I ask you something?"

"Why of course dear."

"Will I have any children?"

The fortune teller began to wave her hands around the ball again, this time closing her eyes and moving her arms wildly as if trying to summon from the depths of the ball an answer that was just as seemingly pleasing as the rest of the spun story.

"Why yes, I do see something."

"What is it?" I asked, trying to join in on the make-believe tale being told.

"I see two shadows. They are coming into view just now. I believe they are; I believe that they are two girls!"

Isabella wiped a tear from her eye as she turned and looked up at me with a big smile on her face. In a way, I hoped that the vision was real. I wanted nothing more than for Isabella to feel complete and happy, and I knew that having children was always something that she had desired. It was a conversation that we had and something that we were going to begin planning to work towards once we got back from our honeymoon. Neither of us wanted to wait.

"Is that it?" Isabella asked the fortune teller.

"Why yes dear. Unless you have any other questions?"

"Do you do palm readings too?" I asked.

The lady looked at me, her eyes growing suspicious for a moment before turning to look at Isabella who was now looking at her intrigued. I knew that Isabella enjoyed the reading with the crystal ball. Perhaps a little something extra could make the night even more memorable.

"It is getting rather late," the woman said, seeming reluctant as she put a small cloth over her ball and slid it across the table.

I reached into my pocket and put some money on the table.

The woman looked down at it before looking back up at me. After a few seconds, she nodded her head and then turned to Isabella and outstretched her hands.

"Place your hands in mine, my child," she informed.

Isabella slowly stretched out her hand, the older woman's eyes immediately jumping to Isabella's large ring, but she tried her best not to make it noticeable. Once Isabella's hands were in hers, she closed her eyes, and her body suddenly went stiff as her eyes seemed to roll back into her head. The woman began to breathe heavily as she quickly let go of Isabella's hands and clutched her own, looking back and forth between us as if suddenly alarmed by something.

"What is it? What's wrong?" Isabella asked, now distressed.

"I saw, no. I can't. It is late."

"Please, you must tell me! I must know what you saw!"

The woman sighed as she looked into Isabella's eyes.

"I saw blood and death, and imminent danger coming in both of your futures."

"Excuse me?" I asked, shocked and appalled that she would say such a thing and especially after I had given her some money.

Isabella stood up and ran outside as tears flowed from her eyes.

I looked at the woman angrily as the woman slid the money across the table as if to hand it back.

"Keep it," I said in an angry tone as I stormed out after Isabella and found her outside.

I put my hand on her back and rubbed it as she turned and gave me a tight hug.

"I don't want anything bad to happen to us. What could she have meant by those words?"

"I don't think she meant anything. You know most of these fortune tellers are phonies. And remember, she did say she saw two little girls in your future. You can't be having any children if anything bad is to happen right?"

Isabella leaned away from me for a moment, and her tears suddenly stopped as she let out a little laugh and smiled.

"Maybe you're right Victor."

Suddenly Isabella's stomach growled loudly and we both let out a laugh.

"I think it's about time I find you some food before this place closes down. What do you say?"

She nodded, and then we both grabbed hands and followed a passing couple who seemed to know where they were going.

Chapter 3

The couple we had followed had, to our luck, been in search of the food area as well.

By the time that we had arrived the sun had completely set, and it was now dark out with the lights of the carnival lighting up the night sky. As Isabella put it in between the monstrous bites she took of her pizza, it was very romantic and beautiful. I too had gotten a slice of pizza, and we both sat while we people watched and just enjoyed all the sights and sounds of the environment around us.

"Oh no!" Isabella suddenly shouted as she jumped up and frantically began to look all around.

"What is it?" I asked concerned, jumping up to help her look for something unaware of what I was looking for.

"My ring!" she cried as she stuck her hand out in front of me, the large diamond of her ring now missing. "The diamond is gone! I don't know where it could be. Oh, Victor, I'm so sorry!"

"Why are you sorry?" I asked as I looked all around the table and in the dirt beneath our seats.

"How could I be so careless? I can't believe this."

"Shh relax. We will find it. Do you remember when you last saw it?" I inquired knowing full well that she would have noticed if it was missing before.

"The last time I remember looking down at my ring was back when we were at the old fortune teller's tent."

I shouldn't have been surprised. The old lady was eyeing it up when she first saw it. I wouldn't be surprised if she somehow loosened it when she was holding onto Isabella's hands and took it. Maybe that was why she slid the money back across the table to me.

"We will find it. Don't worry baby," I consoled as Isabella hugged me and began to weep. "We will make our way back and retrace our exact steps and see if we can find it. Okay?"

She nodded as she wiped the tears from her eyes trying not to make any more of a scene than we already had.

"Let's go," I said as I took her by the hand and led her away from the food area.

Everything looked so much different now that the sun was gone. We walked around for a few minutes, keeping our eyes on the ground as we eventually found the way that we had taken earlier when following the other couple from before. Keeping our eyes out for the fortune teller's tent, we made our way in between other tents and made sure that we were following the same path.

"There it is!" Isabella cried out as she pointed ahead to the tent that had "Fortune Teller," hanging up on top of it.

We charged forward, with me leading the way directly towards the tent until I was suddenly grabbed from the side and came to a complete stop. I turned to see who was grabbing my arm and met the gaze of one of the large, intimidating men that had been standing at the front gate earlier in the day. He towered over me, the cigar still in his mouth, and pulled me away from the tent.

"Gates are closing, time to leave."

"We just want to go inside and look around. My wife lost a part of her ring."

"Don't care," he returned coldly.

"We will only be just a moment. Please?" Isabella asked as she then grabbed the man's arm that was holding onto mine.

He then pushed her away and she stumbled to the ground.

"Hey!" I shouted as I ran over to check if she was okay. "Fucking asshole what's the matter with you?"

Just then the man stepped forward and raised his other arm, a large club grasped firmly in his monstrous hand.

"Stop!" Isabella pleaded, causing the man to stop and lower his arm. "We are going. We don't want any trouble."

I looked back at Isabella with a questioning look on

my face.

"It's okay. We can come back tomorrow," Isabella whispered as she slowly stood up and brushed herself off.

The man pointed and began to slowly walk towards us, pushing us in a specific direction.

We continued to do what he wanted and stuck together as he stayed close behind us and followed. We walked in between tents and then back onto a path where several other families were also walking in a similar direction. We followed them with the large man still close behind, eventually arriving at the front gates, and then exited the circus, turning to look back. The man was standing with his arms crossed in the entrance and was surely not going anywhere until we were out of sight.

"Come back in the morning," he said.

"We'll be back," I fibbed as I put my arm around Isabella and began to walk away with her.

I knew that if we were coming back in the morning that the chances of finding her diamond were long gone if there even was even any chance left as it was.

We continued to follow other families up the street until the front entrance of the circus was now no longer in view. I quickly ducked behind a bush and then pulled Isabella in with me, who was confused at first as to what I was doing.

"I'm not leaving without getting you that diamond back. I'm going to sneak back inside and try and find it. I refuse to wait until tomorrow morning to go back to that old lady's tent. I'm not going to let her get away with this."

"You're not going alone," she decided as she placed both of her hands on my cheeks. "It's too dangerous, and we aren't even sure if she did take it. So, I'll look inside while you look outside. I'll stand out in this dress, so being inside will be for the best."

"We could always go back to the hotel and change," I suggested.

Isabella shook her head no and then stood up with a fierce determination in her eyes. There was no stopping her when she got like that. In fact, there wasn't really any stopping her when she went about doing anything. I wanted her diamond back just as much as she did, but I didn't want her to be in any danger either.

"Let's wait over there," Isabella said as she pointed out a bench in a small park not too far away.

Once we arrived at the bench and took a seat, I turned around. I could still see the circus from where we sat. I knew that if we were going to sneak in, that we probably weren't going to be able to go right through the front gates. I was sure that they would be closed and locked, so we needed to try and find another way inside.

"Hey," Isabella said softly, the tone of her voice soothing amidst the chaotic stress of the moment.

I turned to look at her as she was leaning in and had

both hands on her lap.

"If we don't find it, it's okay, really. At the end of the day, it's just a rock. You're more important to me Victor than any ring ever could be so please, don't blame yourself."

I nodded.

"I just really want to find it. I'm hoping it's still in that tent somewhere. Or if we can find that lady, maybe she has it on her."

"I know you have it set in your mind that she took it, but we don't know that for sure. Before we go in there, I need you to promise me something."

"What is it?" I asked curiously, wondering what she possibly could want me to promise her.

"I want this to be a quick in and out. I don't want to be in there for too long, and I don't want us to get into any trouble. If we see anyone by the tent, get any bad feelings, or can't find it, promise me that we will just leave."

I stared into her big blue eyes for only a brief second before I gave in. I didn't want to leave without finding it, but I knew that she was more important to me than a diamond.

"Say it," she pleaded.

"I promise," I returned.

She smiled and then stretched her legs out as she turned and rested on my lap. I placed my hand on her head as we both looked out towards the lights of the town. Cars drove by, and the movie theater looked as if it had a line stretching out of the door. I wasn't sure if it was to buy tickets, or if everyone was just waiting until it was time to go in and find a seat.

"I wonder what they're all going to see?" Isabella pondered out loud.

"I don't know. It must be a good show though if it's bringing that many people."

***

We sat on the bench for at least an hour. The line of people out front of the theater diminished over time as they went inside. When there was no one left, we both got up and turned to look back at the circus. Most of the lights were off now. I could still see the big tent off in the distance, but a lot of the lights that seemed to be going from tent to tent were now off. Even if we did manage to get spotted, we weren't from around here. We could leave tonight and never see any of these people ever again for the rest of our lives, and I was mentally prepared for that if it came to it. I wasn't going to have some thieves in a carnival steal from us and get away with it, and I surely wasn't going to let either of us get into any trouble trying to steal it back. No one here could recognize us.

"Ready?" Isabella asked as she grabbed my hand, her fingers tightly squeezing in between mine.

"Let's go."

We walked through the rest of the park and then

ducked down behind some bushes until we were close enough to the front entrance to see if anyone was nearby. We didn't see anyone, but we could see that the gates were closed and that the podium that a man had been standing at earlier in the day had been dragged inside.

"We have to find another way in."

"What about over there?" Isabella asked, pointing to a tree not too far away.

I knew what she was thinking and quickly grabbed her face and kissed her.

"Brilliant," I whispered as I took her hand and we carefully made our way over.

The tall tree had a thick branch that went right over the top of the iron-wrought fence. Climbing the fence itself would have been impossible, but the tree gave us a way to go right over.

"I'll help you up first, and then I'll drop down inside and catch you," I instructed.

Isabella agreed, and with my help, she was able to climb up the tree and sit on top of the branch that hung over the fence. While she kept an eye out for anyone while up there, I climbed up next and then carefully moved around her until I was at the end of the branch. I took a glance around to make sure that I didn't see anyone and then dropped down between two tents and a portable popcorn machine. Isabella then scooted herself along the branch and then carefully dropped down into my arms.

"My heart is racing so fast right now Victor."

"Mine too. Let's not make trespassing our new hobby." I joked, causing Isabella to cover her mouth so she didn't let out a chuckle.

"Do you remember which way it is from here?" she asked as we carefully looked out onto the path to see if anyone was coming.

It was clear.

"I think it's this way," I said as I held onto her hand and we ran across the path and in between several tents on the other side. "Yep, it's definitely this way."

 # Chapter 4

***They just had to be hallucinations. They had to
be. Right?***

We carefully moved from tent to tent, making sure
that we didn't make any noise, and spoke only in
whispers. Only one person had come into view, but
they disappeared into a tent further down one of the
paths that we ran across and had no idea that we were
there. Several tents had snoring coming from within,
so we made sure that we were extra careful whenever
we heard that. Before we knew it, we managed to find
ourselves back at the fortune teller's tent. We stayed
hidden behind another tent nearby listening to see if
we could hear anything, but there was nothing. If
someone was inside, we were only going to find out
once someone went in.

Isabella went out first and then headed towards the
entrance while I began to search the ground outside.
She hesitated only for a moment before blowing me a
quick kiss as she disappeared into the darkness within.

The ground was dirt. In a way, it made finding the
diamond even more difficult because if the diamond
got too dirty, then nobody was going to see it. The

moon was now high up in the sky, however, so a small part of me was hoping that the moonlight would reflect off the diamond and cause it to stand out to me.

Minutes passed as I continued to check the entire area outside for a third and then fourth time while Isabella was still inside the tent. That was when I decided that it was time to go in and get her, but just as I turned to head towards the entrance, I heard a scream ring out from far off in the distance. A second later it occurred again, and I recognized that it was coming from the direction of the big tent that we were thankfully nowhere near.

"What was that?" I heard Isabella whisper from the darkness of the tent as she then came into view, empty-handed.

"I don't know. It came from the big tent. No luck?" I asked as I looked down at her hands and then up to her sorrow-filled eyes.

She shook her head no.

"There was a backroom, but I heard snoring coming from inside. I didn't want to make too much noise."

"I'll go in," I said, determined as another scream sounded out only this time a male.

"I'll keep watch, hurry!" Isabella whispered as I darted into the fortune teller's tent.

The table inside looked just the same as when we had left earlier, my money still sitting on top of the table and the crystal ball still beneath a cloth.

I looked around frantically to see if I could find any containers in plain view, but there wasn't much in the room with the table other than some shelves with jars full of dead animals and other weird mystical-looking contraptions.

That was when I noticed the snoring coming from the back room.

I snuck forward as cautiously as I could, carefully pushing several dangling strings of beads to the side until I was on the other side.

It was a small room with a small bed tucked in the corner beside a large chest and dresser. On the bed was the older woman sound asleep and facing the other direction and still wearing her dirty-looking clothes from earlier. If she had it on her, there was no way that I was going to be able to get it back without disturbing her. I took a few glances around the room but again, nothing stood out to me.

It could be anywhere.

After another few seconds of looking around, I gave up and headed back to the dangling beads, but then suddenly as I was about to push them aside, the old lady's snoring came to a stop, and she rolled over in her bed. I looked over my shoulder at her hoping that she was just rolling over, but her eyes were wide open, and she was looking directly at me.

Just then Isabella let out a scream from out front.

"Isabella!" I shouted as the old lady jumped out of her bed and I ran through the tent and then out front.

Isabella was standing out front, but she wasn't alone. The big guard that had been at the gate and then escorted us out of the park had his arms wrapped tightly around her. He had one of them around her waist and the other holding her head with his hand over her mouth, tears flowing from her eyes as she let out muffled screams.

"Let her go!" I shouted as I took a step forward and he took a step back, squeezing her face harder than he already was. "Please don't hurt her!" I begged.

"I told you morning." The towering behemoth said. "You no listen."

"You wouldn't listen to us!" I shouted at him as the old fortune-teller exited the tent and was now standing beside me.

Suddenly Isabella bit the man's finger and then turned and kneed him in the balls. He reacted to the bite, but the knee did nothing to him. He stood over her and then swung his hand at her, hitting her in the side of the face and sending her flying several feet away as she crashed into the ground just in front of me, several teeth and blood falling into the dusty dirt below.

I let out a wild scream, knowing that I was no match for the giant but filled with rage that he hurt her. I ran forward towards him but not even two steps into my attack I was hit from behind and knocked to the ground.

Laughter broke out and I rolled over to see what

was happening.

Two clowns stood over me as two more and the other giant from the gate earlier in the day stepped out of the shadows behind them. The clowns all laughed, joined in by the old lady who rubbed her hands together and then turned to the giant that struck Isabella.

"Take them to the big top!" she yelled in glee as she then burst out into a maniacal laugh.

Two of the clowns picked Isabella up by the arms and then began to drag her away as the other two quickly grabbed me and started to pull me after. I tried resisting, and I tried to break free, but their grasps were too powerful, and both the giants were with us, so I knew to try to fight all of them was just impossible and foolish.

We were both at their mercy, and I didn't know what to do.

The big top grew closer as we continued to get escorted towards it. The old lady sang in a foreign tongue as she walked beside us, turning to look at me every so often with a big smile. All I wanted to do was break free from the still giggling clown's grasp and get my hands on the old lady. I knew that she had the diamond and that she was just messing with us the entire time.

"Where do you want them?" one of the giants said as more screams rang out from the inside of the tent, both male and female.

"Tie them up out back," she ordered as she pointed to two poles on the other side of the big top.

"Let us go, please!" I shouted as the old lady stayed where she was, and the clowns continued to take us away. "We promise never to come back! We only wanted to find the diamond in her ring!"

The old lady laughed again, acting like she didn't care at all as she disappeared out of view and we were brought around the side of the tent towards the poles. First, they tied me up. My arms were outstretched to my sides before they changed their minds and tied them behind me. Isabella was next. As they brought her over to the pole, she punched one of the clowns in the nose and he let out a scream as blood began to pour from it.

"Bitch broke my nose!" he yelled as the other clowns all broke out into laughter.

"Talk about a punch line," another said causing the giants to burst into laughter too.

Isabella stood there and reached down for one of her heels, quickly taking it off and then throwing it at another clown. One of the giants stepped closer to her and grabbed her by the back of the neck and threw her to the ground.

"Isabella no! Leave her be!" I shouted as the giant that threw her to the ground then walked over and kicked her in the stomach.

She rolled over and threw up as the clowns began to grab each of her limbs and hold them outstretched.

The giant dropped his pants and then got down on his knees and got on top of her as she squirmed and tried to break free.

"Stop," a male voice ordered before the giant could even do anything to Isabella.

It was the ringleader of the circus who was the main entertainer.

"You know that kind of behavior isn't welcomed near the big top. This is sacred ground," he said, and the giant quickly stood up and pulled his pants back up, and then lowered his head as he backed away.

With one flick of his hand the ringleader signaled for the clowns to step away from her and then he walked over and knelt beside her.

"Th-thank you," Isabella coughed out as she lowered her dress and covered herself.

"Sometimes they forget their place in all of this. So, forgive them. They have the minds of children."

"Children don't do that," I said, spitting in his direction. "Let us go, and we won't contact the police. We just want to go home."

"I'm sure you do, but what guarantees do I have of this? You lied to one of us already about leaving and here you are, back inside our home and hurting my people."

"We are on our honeymoon. She lost the diamond to her ring. All we wanted to do was find that. We were going to leave as soon as we did."

He nodded, taking off his big hat and running his

white-gloved hand through his turquoise-colored hair before putting his hat back on.

"I am so sorry for this my dear," he said as he turned back to Isabella.

Suddenly, he pressed a button, and a blade came out of a cane that he had been holding in the other hand. He quickly thrust his hand forward and stabbed Isabella in the side, turning the blade slightly as he smiled, and she let out a scream before falling over unconscious from the pain.

"No! How could you!" I cried.

The ringleader quickly stood up and put his knife away, brought his hand up to his mouth, covering it with a single finger before letting out a sadistic laugh. He then pointed to the clowns and then the pole before walking away with the two giants. The clowns looked at me and then one of them raised his hand and punched me in the face causing everything to immediately go black.

# Chapter 5

I don't know how long I was out for, but when I woke, Isabella was still lying on the ground where she had been earlier. I picked my head up and looked around to see if anyone else was nearby, but we seemed to be alone for now.

"Isabella?" I whispered out to her, but she didn't answer.

I called out several more times to her before I thought I saw her move a little.

She did.

Isabella slowly began to roll over. When she did, I was able to see that her shirt was covered in blood from her wound, but at least she was still alive. I didn't know how bad of shape she was in, but she looked like she had lost a lot of blood and I needed to get her out of here and to go get help as soon as possible.

I looked down and tried to get a view of the ropes that were binding my hands. The rope was thick and too tight and cutting off the circulation to my hands as I was getting a pins and needles kind of feeling in them. It seemed that the more I struggled, the tighter they became so I stopped fighting and focused my gaze back onto Isabella.

She had slowly gotten herself into a sitting position now and was looking around, confused and in a daze.

"Isabella," I beckoned; catching her attention as she slowly turned and looked in my direction.

"Vi-Victor?" she replied, her voice both weak and frail.

"Yes, honey it's me. I need you to listen to me and very carefully. I need to get you out of here, but I need you to help me get free first."

She stared at me for a moment before slowly nodding her head yes. I kept looking around to keep an eye out to make sure that nobody was watching, but if someone was, I certainly couldn't see them. Isabella slowly began to crawl over towards me. When she got closer and then slowly rose to her feet, I could see that her face was terribly swollen. She was missing several of her front teeth, and her one eye was almost swollen completely shut, but yet she continued to be a fighter.

"My hands are tied behind my back. See if you can loosen the ropes, but hurry. I don't know how much longer we have until someone comes by."

She nodded and then disappeared behind me as I could feel her hands beginning to play with the ropes. I tried to help by moving my hands but she grabbed them with hers and held them for a moment signaling me that it wasn't helping, so I stopped. I focused again on the area around us, keeping my eyes peeled for any signs of movement or for anything that could potentially help us escape. We had used the tree to climb over the fence to get in, but I had no idea how we were going to get out. The gates were locked, and I wasn't sure how much strength Isabella had left. Our escape needed to be quick and we needed to hurry.

I could suddenly feel the blood rush back into my hands as I found myself able to move them more freely. Seconds later I no longer felt the rope and flung my arms around and back in front of me as I looked down at the rope marks on my wrists.

"Oh thank god," I said aloud as I quickly turned to check on Isabella.

She was standing with one hand on her wound and leaning to the side with the other hand resting on the pole.

"It's time to get out of here," I whispered to her as I quickly put her arm around my shoulder as I began to carry most of her weight.

We began to slowly walk forward, making sure that it was still clear before we moved over to a more shadowed corner in the area in the back of the tent. There were a bunch of wooden pallets and a few bags of what looked like sand that were piled up. We took a short rest to compose ourselves for the long journey back. The only way out I could think of was to try and get back to the tree. I was going to think of a way to get over the fence once we got there, but I didn't have the time to waste to look for another way out now. If I came up empty-handed then I will of only wasted precious time, and that was the valuable time that Isabella might not have.

"Okay, here we go," I whispered as we looked into each other's eyes for a second before we both grimaced and I helped her up.

We moved around a side of the tent that we hadn't been on before and listened carefully as laughs and screams could be heard coming from the inside of the tent. There was a fierce animalistic growl that sounded out before several more screams filled the air. I didn't want to wait to see what was happening, so we kept moving until we turned a corner and saw the back of a clown.

He was standing no more than a dozen yards away but was looking down at another person. It was a younger woman or a teenage girl. It was too dark to tell, but she had one of her hands up in the air and was pleading with him not to take her inside.

"Food for the tigers you'll be, but not before I have my fun with you!" he laughed.

Suddenly he lifted his arm, revealing a machete in his hand, and then swung down at her extended arm. He struck her in the hand, splitting it directly down the middle from the side of the middle finger all the way down to her wrist. She clutched her arm and let out an agonizing blood-curdling scream as he swung several more times at her. Her screams continued until they were diminished into nothing but gurgles as she slowly drowned in her own blood.

The clown let out a big laugh as he knelt over her and then began to make a sawing motion with the machete. Seconds later he rose to his feet again, clutching her blonde hair-covered head in the one free hand that he had remaining.

"Take this one inside. Give her legs to the tigers and have the butcher clean her organs for tomorrow's feast. I don't want anything to go to waste," a familiar voice said.

It was the ringleader.

"That includes that too," he said.

Suddenly the clown raised the girl's head and looked into her still open eyes. He let out a giggle before sighing and tossing the head inside, the head making a thud-like noise as it rolled on the ground. The clown then picked up the girl's legs and dragged the body inside as the ringleader closed a curtain and the side of the tent closed.

"What the fuck," I whispered underneath my breath.

I looked over at Isabella who was looking at me. She smiled, somehow, through the pain and horror of what was happening around us. It seemed we weren't the only ones trapped inside the circus. I didn't know if other people had snuck back inside, or if a few people had been taken against their will, but they were feeding people to the animals and were saving some for them too.

I felt sick to my stomach but now had even more motivation to get us both out of here.

I took a deep breath before we were on the move again. Isabella hobbled, one heel still on as she continued to apply pressure to her wound. I stayed focused on the path ahead, trying desperately to look around for another possible route of escape just in case, but nothing stood out to me. The fence was too tall to climb, and Isabella wasn't going to be strong enough to pull herself up, even with my help. We needed something like a ladder or a car or something.

"Hey!" a voice called out.

I froze and came to an immediate stop. I looked over my shoulder to see if the voice was directed at us and saw a clown back by the tent waving at us.

"Where are you taking that one?" he shouted. "Don't you know we are to bring all of the live ones here? They make for better food when filled with fear!"

I didn't know what to do. We were spotted, but the clown didn't know that I wasn't one of them.

I closed my eyes as I rose my one arm up and waved back, then turning and continuing to hobble forward with Isabella towards a small group of tents. I wasn't sure if the clown was going to follow and see what was going on or if he just figured I was having some twisted fun first. Either way, I needed to keep us moving.

We passed by several tents and then entered inside

of one as Isabella began to grow heavier. I lowered her down onto a bench that was inside and sat beside her as we both tried to catch our breath. She was continuing to grow weaker, and I was using up most of my energy trying to carry most of her weight. Our time was quickly running out.

"You, you need to leave me," Isabella said as she glanced down at her wound.

"No," I returned sternly. "I'm not leaving you here."

She then raised her bloody hand and placed a single finger on my lips and mouthing a shoosh.

"You must. I've lost too much blood. Even if we get out of here, by the time we get help, it will be too late for me, and I'm just holding you back."

She was breathing heavily and pausing in between every couple of words. I could see it in her eyes that she had given up, but I wasn't going to accept that. I wasn't giving up. Not yet.

"I'm not leaving you. I love you. We are going to both get out of here one way or another."

She lowered her head and sighed as the sudden noise of a branch breaking outside could be heard. I quickly jumped to my feet and approached the front of the tent to see if someone was coming. Was it the clown? Did he follow us?

I quickly peered outside and ducked back in, not seeing or noticing anything out of the ordinary. I walked slowly back towards Isabella, maintaining focus on the front of the tent to make sure that someone wasn't going to come rushing in.

Then I felt myself walk into something and come to a complete stop. I turned around and was staring directly into the chest of one of the giants who had somehow snuck in through the back of the tent.

I slowly looked up at him as he stared down at me, his chin several inches above the top of my head. He suddenly grabbed me by the throat and picked me up several feet off the ground. I looked over his shoulder at Isabella who was half bent over and clutching her wound. She was looking up at me and mouthing "I love you," but I only saw her say it once before she suddenly disappeared out of view as I was now flying backward through the air.

I crashed onto the ground outside, landing on my back and knocking all the wind out of my lungs. As I fought to regain air, the giant dragged Isabella out with his hand around her neck. He tossed her to the side as he then rose his foot up and rested it on my chest, slowly pressing down and causing several ribs to break. I screamed as I looked over at Isabella who was watching on in horror. Soon dozens of figures appeared, from clowns to other strange-looking individuals and the other giant.

That was when I could hear a familiar laugh coming from within the crowd.

It was the old fortune teller's laugh.

I screamed at her as the giant continued to press his foot down harder on my chest. I tried desperately to push his foot off, but it didn't budge at all.

The old lady walked over as I noticed the ringleader appear as well. He began to point in several directions, and several clowns then disappeared out of view only to return seconds later with a bunch of rope in hand. They moved behind me and began to throw the rope over a nearby lamppost. I didn't know what they were doing or what they were planning, but it didn't look good for us whatever it was.

"You should have listened," The old lady's voice said as I turned and looked up at her grinning face. "You should have come back tomorrow. You wouldn't have witnessed what you both did tonight, and both of you wouldn't be suffering as you are. I warned you of what I saw."

Suddenly a clown appeared out of breath from in between two tents and held out his hand behind the old woman saying that he found it. She turned and looked at his hand and then grabbed something before turning back around to look at me. Her smile faded, and her expression turned to sorrow as she held up her hand, Isabella's diamond glistening in between her fingers.

Isabella was right. The old lady didn't have the diamond after all.

"Such a shame. Young love. Filled with such passion, but blind you both it did."

"Pl-please," I pleaded as I was suddenly grabbed, lifted to my feet, and then pulled over to the lamppost.

A rope suddenly found its way around my neck as I was raised upwards and my throat began to get crushed by the weight of my body. I fought against it as I looked down at the old lady, the world becoming slightly fuzzy.

"You should have listened. You and your love would still be alive tomorrow if you did."

That was when I realized that her vision during the palm reading had turned out to be true.

I looked in Isabella's direction and reached out to her, and she reached out to me. I tried to scream out to her, but I was unable. The last thing that I saw was Isabella being dragged away by her hair by one of the giants, accompanied by two clowns that were both carrying machetes. Their wicked and wild laughter was the last thing I heard as the world faded away to black and my body became numb as I lost consciousness.

Isabella.

Part Two

Chapter 6

"All you have to do is follow me."

"I'm trying, sir."

"I'm not asking you to try!" he yelled as he slammed his fists on the edge of the vanity. "I'm asking you to just fucking listen to me and follow my god damn lead. That's it. Nothing less and nothing more."

"Yes, sir."

"Good. Obedience is all that I request. I know that you're new to our crew, but I am not the ringleader of this band of twisted miscreants for nothing. Some people I give one chance, some two, and some get none. So do not fuck up and pay attention. So, one more time, from the top."

"I'm ready."

"I will head out from behind the cages into a darkened interior of the tent. Once there, you will turn the spotlight on and moved it wildly across the crowd and have it end on me, center stage, and in the middle of the big top. Then I will give my speech and welcome the crowd. Whenever I point my cane in a direction, move the spotlight to reveal the next act as it comes out. I want dramatics, grandeur, and the audience to never expect what's coming next. That is why every show must be different. An old show is a dead show."

"Is that why the circus is always moving?"

Suddenly the ringleader stopped powdering his face and turned away from his mirror.

"There's another reason for that. You will come to find out soon enough."

The ringleader then turned back and began to apply his lipstick, pausing momentarily to let out a dark and devilish chuckle.

"And if you choose to leave after you find out our little secret here. I'll just feed you to the cats. Or maybe to the clowns," he announced but in a tone that was hard to differentiate whether he was serious or being sarcastic.

"I'm sure whatever it is I can manage."

"You better. My last assistant had a misfortunate event occur after he challenged me on something. I would hate to see such talent go to waste."

"If I may ask, what was it? You're the boss, so I want to make sure I don't overstep."

The ringleader paused mid-motion while applying his eyeliner and looked at the assistant in the mirror. He stared at him for a moment before smiling and then continued applying his makeup.

"You'll know if you overstep. As I said before, just follow my lead. Do what I ask without question, watch, learn, and you'll fit in just fine."

The assistant nodded still unsure of what to make of

it all.

"So, tell me your story kid, not that I really care. At the end of the day, however, I'd like to know who I have running around here and who was fighting my clowns."

The assistant nodded before clearing his throat.

"I'm a runaway."

"No shit," the ringleader said. "I can tell by what you're wearing. You've got nicer clothes on than a bum, but you're also too young to have truly faced life. Did you steal something? Murder someone? Did you get kicked out by your old man?"

"None of those things," he replied. "I just ran away. I don't know why really. I just woke up and felt like I didn't belong anymore. I was never the favorite, and I didn't have anywhere else to go. I'm only fourteen so a lot of places won't hire me. I'm also not that strong, so I'm not great for physical labor."

"Well, you know how to scrap that's for sure. Either that or my clowns are just idiots and underestimated you. You knocked two of them out before you got overwhelmed. If I didn't hear the commotion and step in, you'd surely be dead by now."

"Thank you for stopping them," the assistant said.

"Continue with your story. I'm intrigued. Why did you come here?"

"I don't know. I saw that everything was being packed up and I thought I could just sneak in and hide. I thought maybe if I wasn't found right away, I could travel with you all to someplace new and get off there or stay."

"Well, as stupid as you are for leaving whatever life it is you did have, you're my assistant now as you already know. It's the only job I could give you that would make you untouchable by the others. Anything else is free reign. If I put you in with the clowns, you'd be dead before I even left the room. I can't put you as a guard, because you're too small, which will change over time. You will become stronger. I'll make sure of that. I can't put you with the animals because you're inexperienced and I can't risk one of them getting out and eating a bunch of my crew. So now you have the second hardest job under the big top and the smallest of margins to fuck it up. How does that make you feel?"

The assistant shrugged his shoulders and didn't respond, unsure of what he was really feeling about it. He knew that it was better than being dead, but he had no idea of what was going to be getting asked of him in the future. He knew that he had to follow the ringleader and do whatever he asked without questioning him, but what did that entail really? Besides overseeing the spotlight to start, was he going to be in charge of other things around the circus? Was he going to be in charge of people too? Was he really safe and untouchable in his position?

"Who's the boy?" an elderly woman's voice asked as a shadow appeared in the entrance of the ringleader's tent.

"My new assistant."

The old lady walked in slowly and came to a stop beside the boy, looking him up and down suspiciously before chuckling.

"Oh, what a future you're going to have here. I can see it now," she said as she placed her hands on the boy's cheeks and examined his swollen and cut-up face. "Much violence and darkness inside of this one. Lots of anger."

"Leave him be woman," the ringleader said as he stood up from behind his vanity and walked over, the candlelight reflecting off his almost clown-like-looking face. "How do I look?"

"You kind of look like that clown from those comic books."

The ringleader glanced back at his reflection in the mirror for a second before quickly turning back and placing his hand on the boy's shoulder.

"He's got nothing on me kid," he said as he walked past him and exited the tent, motioning for the boy to follow him.

When the boy exited the tent, followed closely by the old lady, the ringleader was standing out front and looking out over the concourse.

"What's your name?"

"Christo-"

"Wait, let me rephrase that," the ringleader interrupted. "What do you want to be known by?" he inquired as he turned and looked at the boy. "Who you were is dead. Think of this as a rebirth."

"I-I don't know. Something cool I guess?" the boy replied unsure of himself.

"Jug. I am going to call you jug," the ringleader determined.

"Jug?"

"Yes. I am going to call you jug because I am going to fill you with so much knowledge and power that you will become the embodiment of all my ideas. You will learn everything that there is to know about our little circus here." The ringleader then began to wave his arms around and point his cane in various directions. "You will learn everyone's purpose here. You will grow, become stronger, and I am going to bring out things inside of you that you didn't even know existed there."

Jug nodded and as odd as he thought the name was, he also kind of liked it. He was a new person now, and even though he was still unsure about himself, he was being given an opportunity to be a part of something bigger than just himself.

"Now, let me officially take you around and introduce you to everyone before we get these gates open for tonight's show."

Jug followed the ringleader as they began to head across the concourse. They passed the food area and several tents that were being used for shops and selling other types of small trinkets. Next, they began to head towards some bigger blue tents where two large hulking men stood up and welcomed the ringleader as he entered inside.

"This is Mason and Ace. They guard the gates and deal with anyone unlucky enough to stir up any trouble here."

Suddenly they both picked up their massive fists and slammed them into their other hands in a punching motion.

"You don't want to be on the other end of one of those, kid. Trust me on that."

Jug nodded. He continued to look back and forth between the two giants who stared at him with suspicion in their eyes. Even though he was now a part of them, he knew that everyone was going to be wary of him until he proved himself.

After talking for several more minutes with the giants, Jug followed the ringleader out of the tent as they then headed over towards an old-looking brown tent that was hidden behind several other ones. When they entered, Jug pushed aside the beads hanging from the ceiling and entered a room that had a table with something covered sitting on top of it. Suddenly a shadow appeared at the back of the tent. It was moving behind another wall of beads. It looked like it was pacing back and forth until it came to a stop and stepped out, revealing it to be the old lady that had visited the ringleader and placed her hands on Jug's face.

"This is our fortune teller," the ringleader officially

introduced. "Just in case you didn't figure that out from when you met her earlier."

Just as Jug was about to say something to her, she disappeared back into the shadows again. The ringleader shook his head with a chuckle before heading back out of the tent and outside again.

"She's a crazy one," he said. "But she's never wrong."

"Never?" Jug asked.

The ringleader looked over his shoulder at him.

"Never," he repeated before beginning to walk away.

Jug then thought back to how she had said he had a lot of anger, violence, and darkness inside of him. He didn't know what she was talking about, but she did say that he was going to have a future there.

What kind of future that was going to be was still yet to be determined.

After the animals and meeting the kitchen staff, the ringleader took Jug over to the clowns. At first, they were very aggressive, but the ringleader was quick to hit anyone who got too close with his cane to keep them from getting too close to Jug. Once they were reminded who was in charge and to keep their distance, they then began to tease and make fun of Jug because of his name. They kept saying how clown-like it was and that he should join them, but the ringleader was quick to dismiss that he would never be as low as the clowns were.

Jug didn't know what he was talking about, but he was sure he would find out eventually.

Chapter 7

The first show in the new town had gone smoothly. Jug did well with the spotlight, and the ringleader was extremely pleased with his performance. He even gave Jug some money for doing so well. He said that if Jug kept it up, and continued to do well, that after a few shows, he may start to gradually increase not only what he earned, but his actual responsibilities with the show. Eventually, he could even be in the show and have his own act, but that would only be if he had a hidden talent and it was entertaining enough to be used during the live show, or if it was only going to be something that could be used in some side tent.

***

Months passed. More shows in more towns, success after success. Jug was growing, learning, and he was gaining the trust of those around him in the circus. Some of the clowns still had grudges, but he had become good friends with the giants and the old fortune-teller, while still weird, she never had any issues with him. He continued to listen and follow the instructions of the ringleader closely. He listened to everything he taught him about the importance of showmanship, entertainment, maintaining the equipment, and all the inner workings of pushing the crowds towards certain acts or towards the big top by using people in plain clothes.

It was a lot of work, and a lot went into making the circus run as smoothly as it did, but it was fun.

Still, in the back of his mind, Jug was curious. He remembered that the ringleader had mentioned there was some sort of a secret, but he still had no inclination on what it was. He never saw anything that seemed to be too terribly out of the ordinary, for a circus at least. He also never saw anyone do anything bad enough to get themselves turned into cat food.

When the time came that the ringleader said Jug needed to begin to find out what talents he had, he jumped at the chance to prove himself. He did not know what he was going to be good at, but he really wanted to find out, and he was hoping that it was going to be something that could really benefit everyone and the circus as a whole.

They started with the magician. He tried to teach Jug some of the simpler tricks that he knew. He was able to memorize some of them, but it was going to take a lot of practice in order to get good at it, and it wasn't anything that could be of use in the big top, mainly since there already was a magician side act.

Next up was working with the animals. Jug, while reluctant to approach the cats at first, found himself enjoying working with them. He stuck close to the trainer's side and learned different commands and ways to control them and make them do whatever he wanted. Jug found it enjoyable until one of them bit the trainer and ripped his arm off in the process. The clowns and giants were luckily on standby and able to stop them from getting to Jug and killing him too, but for the time being, the animal act had to be suspended until a new trainer stepped up. Jug wasn't ready yet and as much as he wanted to help because the previous trainer had taught him some of the commands, the ringleader didn't want him to be around them because of how unruly they were being.

Jug had wondered what happened after they removed the body of the trainer from where he was killed and torn to shreds, but he never bothered to ask. He watched as the giants carried the mangled body out, his throat torn open and his intestines hanging out. None of it bothered Jug, because he was thinking better the trainer than himself, but he could not get the trainer's face out of his mind for days. Mouth wide open, one eye hanging out of the socket because of a bite that caved in one side of the head, and the nose completely torn off.

It almost seemed like it was fake, but the trainer's screams and the bloodstain that remained on the grass after the circus began to make its way onto the next town were reminders that it really did happen. That there were dangers to what they were doing, but as the ringleader said to everyone later that night during dinner, the show must go on, and sometimes sacrifices were necessary for the rest of us to learn and grow.

***

As more time passed and a few more shows were under his belt, the ringleader thought it would be good to throw a celebration for Jug. He had now been with them for a little over a year, and it was time for him to be recognized for all the hard work that he was doing. Running the lights, learning the intricacies of the show, helping with setting up and moving, learning the inner workings of the overall circus, being allowed to schedule acts in some of the smaller towns, and helping with marketing and promotions.

The ringleader was impressed and grew fond of Jug, allowing him to even join in during a show once as a random audience member chosen to be used for a trick. While it was a gimmick, it meant a lot to Jug to be able to participate directly in the show itself beyond what he had been doing behind the scenes. It was a monumental moment for him, and he bragged about it for weeks until everyone in the circus had heard the story at least once or twice.

***

"If you could change anything about this circus, what would it be, and why?" the ringleader asked Jug.

Jug sat by and thought about it for a few seconds. There were a few things that he would change, but it wasn't anything serious. He thought carefully about how he was going to respond. He didn't want to say anything that was going to be rude possibly or that the ringleader might take offense to. That was the last thing that he wanted to do, especially after being with the circus for so long and not ever gotten onto the ringleader's bad side, at least not yet.

"I would make it darker," he eventually replied.

The ringleader looked at him for a few seconds with a curious expression on his face, intrigued by Jug's response.

"Darker you say? How so?"

"I'm not sure. Something darker though. I know circuses are supposed to be fun and full of laughter and good times, but what if we held a show that scared people instead? What if instead of them coming here to enjoy themselves, we did something that was full of crazy stunts or things that terrify people and make them jump out of their seats?"

The ringleader's eyes grew bigger for a moment as a smirk crossed his face.

"That is a great idea, but sadly one that I thought up long ago. Life itself is dark and hard. People don't want to pay to get scared or horrified when their daily lives already give that to them. They want an escape. Laughter, tears, fun. That's what drives a good circus."

Jug agreed, but in secret, he held onto his idea. He suddenly became obsessed with it even. He thought that perhaps one day, once he learned enough and perhaps had enough money, he could somehow start his own circus and have it exactly how he wanted it to be. He understood and could see the ringleader's point of view. Jug knew that he was right that life itself was hard and people wanted an escape that was going to be pleasant and not terrifying, but in a way, he thought that perhaps people experiencing some sort of a terrifying event but in a safe and controlled environment might end up being more fun or releasing then what they were used to expecting from a circus.

And perhaps it would even draw more attention then.

***

A few more months passed before Jug ended up stumbling upon something after a show. While walking the grounds of the concourse and helping to close the place for the night, he ended up finding what looked like a hole underneath a fence. He wasn't sure if it had always been there, but the way the dirt was pushed it looked like it was relatively recent and like someone or something had climbed under and made its way inside.

Then Jug noticed some footprints in the soft dirt.

Jug followed them. They went in between some of the

tents and then looked spaced apart when they reached out in the open like someone was running or taking bigger steps. Whoever it was is sneaking around and trying not to get caught.

After following them for several minutes, Jug realized that they were headed straight for the ringleader's tent in the back of the circus, so he continued to follow them, curious and suspicious about whose footsteps they were.

As he approached the tent, he saw a tall shadowy figure standing beside it. Not sure if it was someone random, or if it was even who he was tracking down, he watched the shadow for a few seconds while he stayed hidden behind some boxes.

The shadow moved slowly, ducking down whenever someone walked by, and then after pulling something shiny out, it lifted the tarp on the side of the tent and rolled underneath.

Jug quickly ran towards the tent. He didn't know what was happening or what was going on. He didn't even know if the ringleader was even inside, but he had to stop whoever it was from doing whatever they were trying to do.

Upon entering the tent, Jug looked frantically around to see where the shadow had gone, and then that was when he saw it.

The ringleader was sitting at his vanity but was too focused on applying his makeup that he didn't notice the shadow approaching him from behind.

"Look out!" Jug yelled, startling everyone in the tent.

The shadow stopped and looked over towards him while the ringleader looked up and turned to face his attacker, the shiny item a pointed dagger. The shadowy figure suddenly turned and went to stab the ringleader, but the ringleader had pulled a knife out of nowhere and stabbed the person first. They both fell into the vanity and knocked it over with a loud crash. Jug ran forward to try and see if he could help, but the two men wrestled on the ground until the ringleader was up top and holding his knife to the attacker's throat. He pulled off the man's hood, revealing a young-looking man but who appeared to still be older than Jug.

"That was very stupid," the ringleader said to the man as the front of the tent opened and the giants accompanied by some clowns all entered. "Deal with him," the ringleader said as the man screamed and kicked his legs while being dragged away until one of the giants punched him in the face once and knocked him out, all his teeth flying out and landing on the ground in the process.

"Thanks, Jug," the ringleader said as Jug helped him lift his vanity back up.

"No problem. Are you going to be okay?" Jug inquired as he pointed to the ringleader's arm that had a small cut on it but was bleeding.

"I've had worse, much worse. Good thing you came in when you did. I wonder how he got in?" the ringleader said out loud but not directing his question at Jug.

"There was a hole by the fence. I tracked him from there by following his footsteps until I ended up seeing him sneak into the tent."

"You tracked him? Hmm."

The ringleader smiled as he looked at Jug curiously for a moment. A few seconds later he laughed and then clapped his hands together once.

"Well, it seems like you have a talented after all."

"I do?"

The ringleader nodded.

"You can track."

"But all I did was follow his footsteps. It really wasn't that hard."

"Do you know how dark outside it is?" the ringleader said as he signaled for Jug to follow him.

Once they were outside the ringleader pointed to the ground and then up to the sky.

"You can't see a fucking thing out here unless you have a candle and this dirt? This dirt is god awful and dusty. There are hundreds of different tracks and paths that people have been walking all day. The steps by the fence could have led you anywhere. Instead, you were able to follow them directly to their source and saved my life in the process."

Jug was shocked. He was unsure of himself at first, but perhaps the ringleader was right? Maybe he was good at tracking? Perhaps he did have a gift or a talent after all? But how on earth could that be used to benefit the circus? How, in any way, could tracking be used to help bring in money or make the circus any more exciting?

"I have the perfect job for you now Jug. I no longer need you as my assistant. You've already learned all you could about running a circus for the most part anyway. At least what was teachable. The rest is just a combination of creativity and experience."

Jug looked at the ringleader in surprise and was wondering what on earth he had in mind. He thought that being an assistant was as high as he could go. What else was there? Where else was there to go? What other job was there that could be more important than the ringleader's direct assistant?

"I know exactly what I'm going to use you for."

 # Chapter 8

Tracking was exactly what the ringleader had in mind for Jug. The night after the attempted murder, the ringleader took Jug into his tent and sat him down, explaining not only the darker history of the circus, but also what he had been grooming the boy for, and what he now knew was Jug's ultimate purpose.

The ringleader had obtained the circus from his abusive father who was also in the trade. It took decades of hard work and grinding against the much bigger competition to try and scrape together enough money to keep the circus growing and to pay for workers and purchase new equipment. It was a dying form of entertainment and needed a makeover. That was why he eventually overthrew his father and reinvented it. He made it flashy with fancy lights, music, more animals—some of them dangerous—and added in freaks like the giants at the front gates who also doubled as security and the old lady who was somehow old even when he was a young boy and who seemed to never age. He traveled quickly, only staying in towns for a few days, calling it lightning stops. It was hard and grueling work but being able to come and go so quickly allowed the circus to visit places quicker than the competition that stayed in areas for a week or more at a time.

Most of the time they broke even, but if a show was really good, sometimes they were able to scrounge enough money up for something special. They had enemies, however, and not everything was just entertainment and fun.

There was a much darker side to the circus life that he had been shielding Jug from, but now Jug had gotten a firsthand experience, and it was about time that he was told the truth.

There were people out to kill the ringleader. Not just because he was the leader of a small circus of delinquents and outcasts, but because he had something that no other circus currently had.

Real acts.

The animals were real, the fortune teller was real, the freaks and giants were also real.

The competition understood this and if the small circus continued at the pace that it was, it was going to overpass some of the bigger circuses eventually and would only grow bigger and better. The ringleader was trying to stay under the radar as much as he could, making sure not to visit any place twice in a year and nowhere that another circus had recently been. He tried to avoid where they currently were too. The goal was simple, raise the tent in as many small towns as possible and get there before the other bigger ones did. This way when they came around, people might be exhausted and not visit the larger competition, and in turn, this would hurt their finances.

They didn't like that.

It wasn't the first time that his life had been almost taken either. It had happened a few times actually. Once they confused one of the clowns for him, which was one of the reasons why he always wore makeup. They found the clown behind a bunch of barrels with his throat slit ear to ear, and his tongue ripped out from his throat. Another time someone came in but right through the front of the tent. There was not much thought put into it because once they saw that the ringleader was alone, they froze, and it gave him enough time to shoot him.

The ringleader said after that, he did not allow guns on the premises. It was too loud and drew too much unwanted attention. If someone was to cause a scene or try anything again, it had to be dealt with silently. The less attention from local authorities the better.

That was when the ringleader revealed that a third attempt occurred a few months before Jug showed up. He showed up screaming and ranting and raving at the front gates after it was closed. He wanted to create a scene, but the giants quickly took care of him and dragged him inside and then out of view to where they then let the clowns torture him for fun before they cut him into tiny pieces and fed him to the cats.

When Jug was discovered hiding, that's why the clowns attacked. They thought he was just another person trying to sneak in and get their moment, but the ringleader knew that Jug was different and that that wasn't why he was there. That's why he was spared and why he stepped in to stop the clowns from killing him.

After the ringleader was done telling him the back story of the attempts on his life and how the circus came to be, he then told Jug what he had been waiting to hear since he started. He told him what the dark secret was, and that if he chose to leave after, he would not actually hold it against him because of how fond he had grown of him.

"I suppose you never put much thought into what we eat around here do you?" the ringleader asked as he was obviously hesitant while asking the question.

"Not really."

"Do you have a favorite menu item?"

Jug seemed to think for a moment before he nodded his head yes.

"The soup is my favorite I think."

The ringleader lowered his head for a moment before slowly lifting his chin, revealing a twisted smile.

"What about the soup?"

"I like the bits of meat inside. It's just got a different flavor. Why?"

"Have you seen any refrigerators here on our grounds or when we're moving anything around?"

"I don't believe so."

"Don't you find that strange that we have fresh meat every night in our soup and sometimes have bigger meat-related meals once a week?"

Jug scratched the back of his head trying to think hard, but he couldn't think of anything. He had no idea what the ringleader was trying to tell him.

"Leaving the towns so quickly isn't just business tactic. We do it because we don't want anybody to catch on or to find out what we're doing."

"What are we doing?" he asked, still bewildered.

"Jug," the ringleader said as he then leaned forward into the candlelight. "We're all cannibals."

***

Six years passed since that night that the ringleader revealed the dietary surprise of the carnival. Jug had handled it better than he had thought, in fact, he handled it better than the ringleader could ever have imagined. He not only took it and didn't react but in fact, he embraced it. He accepted it and ever since, even enjoyed his meal times even more.

There were no secrets remaining anymore between the ringleader and Jug and life at the circus was good and flourishing, especially for Jug and the new role that he was now years into happily carrying out.

Tracking.

The ringleader helped him get experience in training and honing his natural ability to track people down by sending him out on missions once he thought that he was ready. Jug was being sent out to hunt down those who meant to come and bring harm to their small circus. Whether it was to blend into the bigger circuses and try and catch wind of a murderous plot and end it before it even began, or to send a message to those who were already well-aware of their presence and tried to beat them to the town first.

The first few times Jug didn't know what he was doing, but as time went on and he grew into his new role, he began to become ruthless and cutthroat to those he was hunting down. The other circuses got the messages, and for a while, Jug was feared by even some of the people that he had become close to over the years.

His hair had grown as long and wild as his brutality and his patience as thin as his temper. There were even a few times where the ringleader was even surprised and shocked at Jug's insatiable desire to hunt down anyone who meant to endanger the overall wellbeing of the circus. Sometimes he seemed to enjoy and relish in it a little too much and the ringleader needed to remind him that keeping a low profile was key to surviving and continuing their wildly succeeding streak.

Jug, at times, would even leave the confines of his tent and stay with the clowns, sometimes for days to weeks at a time. They became close to him, and he earned not only their respect but their admiration too. There was something about him that they were attracted to, or perhaps, feared. It wasn't just his bloodlust, but his growing confidence, his charismatic ways that were blossoming and that he was using to really help draw in crowds and get them pumped up during the shows. It was a remarkable difference to how his relationship had changed from when he had first snuck into the circus and got discovered to now years later. He went from being nearly beaten to death by the clowns, to now being looked at as the next best thing.

While the ringleader was growing older, he was still young enough to have many years left in his role in the big top. Jug knew this too, and he looked up to him as a father figure because of everything that he had taught him. While he still was holding onto his own vision of a darker circus full of fear and thrills, he still respected the current methods and abided by them, even if some of the clowns whispered to one another and to Jug in the middle of the night that, one day, the time to overthrow the ringleader as he had done to his own father was coming.

Jug would always denounce the ideas they had and to remind them that saying anything like that out loud was ground for severe punishment or death, but in the back of his mind, it was fuel for the fire and just like the old lady fortune-teller had predicted and seen so many years ago, there was a darkness and violence in him that was strong enough for her to be able to foresee immediately upon meeting him.

There was a darkness building up inside of him, and

even Jug knew that it was only a matter of time before he could not hold it in anymore, but he was not afraid of it. Instead, he fed into it, little by little, cultivated it, nurtured it, and trained himself to be able to hold it off until the time was right for him to allow it to take its course and lead him to his destiny. Before it was time that he could rise and either start his own circus or overthrow the ringleader and take control of the one that he was currently in.

Chapter 9

Two more years passed. Two more years of tracking enemies down and killing them in preemptive strikes. Little did the ringleader know, however, that Jug had stopped killing those who would come and kill the ringleader, because there were none left, at least that he was aware of.

He had struck such fear into the competition that they didn't dare to even think about sending someone after the ringleader. This didn't stop Jug from still paying them visits or killing a person at random just to set an example. Sometimes he was never seen, but they always knew that it was him because of the amount of brutality that his victims would meet.

Now, whenever Jug would leave the confines of the circus at night, the clowns would go with him and together they would begin to take people from the towns they stayed in once the sun was down and everyone was fast asleep. This angered the ringleader once he found out, not only because it was careless and risked exposing the circus and catching the eyes of the authorities, but it also wasn't necessary. They got enough food from those who tried to sneak into the circus at night or those who lingered for just a little too long after the closing announcements and the big show was over.

Eventually, the ringleader had enough and couldn't take it anymore, but he was going to wait until he felt that the time to confront Jug was just right.

**

"You were gone for two whole days this time, Jug. You and the clowns even missed a show," the ringleader said as Jug strolled into the circus one early morning covered in blood from head to toe and with his bat over his shoulders with both arms stretched over.

"I thought we weren't starting until tonight?"

The ringleader stared at him as the clowns continued walking past him, leaving the two of them alone.

"You've been doing this for years now. You know we always start two days after arrival, and we always leave two days after that. We are never in any town for any longer than that."

Jug just stared at him without a response like a child being scolded by his father, however, it instead looked like he didn't even care and that the ringleader's words weren't bothering him one bit.

"Did you hear what I said?" he asked Jug, raising his voice louder than he had anticipated. "We don't fucking miss shows. I needed you, I needed the others, and none of you were here. The show suffered because of it. This is unacceptable."

"It won't happen again," Jug said as he went to go walk around the ringleader so he could go off to his own tent.

Suddenly the ringleader stepped in front of him and grabbed him by the arm.

"You need to stop this, and I need you to focus. You're letting your bloodlust and your palette get the best of you. I can't have this happen again. You of all people should understand that."

Jugs eyes were fixated on the ringleader's hand that was grabbing onto his arm. A few seconds after the ringleader said his words, Jug slowly began to turn his head until his piercing eyes looked into the ringleaders.

This sent a chill down the ringleader's spine and throughout his body. He already knew that Jug was dangerous, and he knew since the very beginning that there was darkness inside of him. This, however, was the first time that he could see it in his eyes to the degree that he did. It was like Jug was peering into the ringleader's very soul and that he could look right through him as if he almost wasn't even there.

It was like staring into the abyss and having it stare back at you.

The ringleader let go of Jug's arm in that instant and took a step away from him as a creepy smile stretched across Jug's face. The ringleader didn't know how to react or what was going through Jug's head, but he was certain that Jug was now no longer under his control.

The ringleader watched as Jug slowly walked away. Once he was out of view, he took a deep breath and then realized that other circus workers had been watching the altercation and had been hiding just out of view.

"Get back to work. All of you!" he shouted as he watched the workers scatter off in every direction and get back to whatever their tasks at hand were.

***

Later that night, after the show, that the clowns and Jug showed up for this time, the ringleader returned back to his tent as he always did once the crowds were gone and the gates were closed. He sat in his chair beside the vanity and stared at his reflection. He slowly began to remove his makeup and once he was done, he sat there looking into his own eyes and picking apart his image in his mind at every new wrinkle that he came across.

Then a thought entered his mind and he looked down at his cane beside the vanity as he became overwhelmed with emotion.

"You don't need to be sad," a voice said from the shadows behind him.

The ringleader gasped and turned, collecting himself once he realized that it was Jug who was coming to pay a visit.

Jug took a few steps further into the tent and was

standing just close enough for the candlelight to illuminate half of his face.

That was when the ringleader noticed that the makeup that Jug had on was different than what he was wearing during the show. In fact, from what he could see, it looked a lot like how he did his own makeup only Jug wasn't using any eyeliner.

"Are you feeling okay?" Jug asked.

The ringleader nodded slowly before turning back to the mirror and staring at Jug's reflection.

"I'm just tired. It's been a long few days."

Jug nodded as he took another small step forward and that was when the ringleader noticed the candlelight reflecting off something metallic in one of Jug's hands. He could not make out what it was because Jug had both of his arms folded together and whatever it was that the light had flickered off of was tucked under his armpit, but even though he didn't get a full glimpse he knew exactly what it was as Jug took another step forward.

"I knew this day would come," the ringleader said with a sigh.

Jug tilted his head as if intrigued by what he was saying.

"The old woman. She foresaw it."

"So, this entire time, you knew?"

The ringleader nodded.

"Then why continue to train me or take me in to begin with? Why not end me right there once you found out?"

"Because, just like my father, retirement isn't an option. Where would I go? What would I do? Look at me, I'm old." The ringleader said as he gently stroked one of his own cheeks with his one hand. "Live and die with the circus. I don't have any children of my own. I had to make sure that I taught you everything that I knew and that I trained you right. That I tested you and pushed you to make sure that you were ready for when the time came. It was always your destiny that you would find this circus and that it would one day become yours. That's why fate led you here that one night all those years ago. I knew you were coming then too. She told me, I was just too prideful to accept it until there you were and in our midst."

The two continued to stare into each other's eyes as silence filled the air. The ringleader knew that Jug was there to kill him, and Jug knew that the ringleader was aware and even prepared for the moment.

"Well then," Jug said as he eventually lowered his arms and revealed that the object that was in his hand was a large knife. "Anything else you want to say?"

The ringleader looked down at his cane beside him one more time before he let out a sigh and then looked back up to meet Jug's gaze in the mirror's reflection.

"This is your final test," the ringleader announced, and with that Jug lunged forward with his knife-wielding hand raised.

In the time that it took Jug to fly through the air

towards him, the ringleader had quickly reached over to grab his cane. As he grabbed it, Jug's hand with the knife slashed by his face but missed. The ringleader then swung his cane around, but Jug grabbed it with his other free hand and held it out to the side while he brought his knife around again to try and stab the ringleader in his side. The ringleader took a step back, now practically sitting on top of the edge of his vanity which caused Jug's knife to slash across his stomach instead of stabbing him in his side.

The ringleader let out a yell as the slash of the blade was deep and he could feel it pierce through his skin and rip open both his stomach and intestines. As the blood immediately began to pour out and onto the floor, the ringleader went to pull on his cane, but Jug was already beating him to it. Jug twisted and jerked the one end of the cane away from the ringleader, pulling the hidden knife out of it and then swinging it across and cutting the ringleader's throat in a single swift motion.

The ringleader let out a gurgle as the blood began to pour out from his throat and in between his fingers and hands that were clutching onto his neck.

Jug smirked as he took a few steps back and watched the ringleader fall to his knees as his intestines spilled out and onto the floor below. His eyes grew large as he looked up to Jug.

"It's all mine. Thank you for teaching me well. I'll make you proud and make this circus even better. It's time for me to do it my way."

The ringleader, while continuing to bleed out, nodded his head once before a smile crossed his dying face. His lips were moving, and he was trying to say something but was struggling as he was rapidly losing blood and only had seconds remaining.

Jug took a small step forward and knelt, bringing himself closer to try and hear what the ringleader was saying.

"The show...must...go on," the ringleader said as he let go of his throat and the blood began to flow freely now.

A second later he fell backward into his vanity and with his back leaning up against it, he continued to look up at Jug with a smile on his face until his body slowly slumped to one side and he closed his eyes and died.

Jug let out a sigh as he stood up. He walked over to the vanity and sat down, reaching for the ringleader's eyeliner pen and then applying it to his eyes. Just as he was finishing the final touches on his makeup and rubbing some color into his hair, staring at his face that looked almost exactly like the previous ringleader now, only a little creepier, he noticed a shadow in the mirror's reflection quickly approaching from behind. He turned around as fast as he could and swung his arm with the knife in the same motion but one of the giants grabbed onto his arm and held it firmly in place. Jug looked up to the giant who took one glance over towards the dead body of the ringleader and then back to Jug.

Suddenly the giant began to pull Jug towards the front of the tent and then tossed him onto the dirt-covered ground outside. Jug was quick to bounce back up to his feet. Mentally he was preparing himself to have to defend himself for what he did, but when the giant just stood at the front of the tent and was no longer coming at him, he looked around and realized that they weren't alone.

Everyone from the circus was surrounding them. The clowns, the animal trainers, the old lady, and the other giant were all staring at Jug as he spun in circles looking at everyone and wondering what was going on.

The giant who had thrown him out of the tent then knelt onto one knee, and everyone else followed suit. Soon, everyone was kneeling while they all bowed their heads to Jug and he realized that they were recognizing and accepting him as their new leader, as their new ringleader.

"The show must go on," the old lady said out loud.

"And it will," everyone else said in perfect unison.

The circus was now his and his alone.

 # Chapter 10

The circus changed and became exactly what Jug had envisioned and wanted it to become. Not only did it continue with its cannibalistic ways behind the scenes, but it became much darker in appearance when the crowds were there for the show. The entire environment was much more electric because Jug changed it from being a fun and safe family type of an event to a show filled with death-defying stunts and acts, dark humor, and plenty of cheap thrills that got the audience to jump and scream.

Jug was right. His ideas would resonate with people, and they would come in even more now because of how much different it was than how it used to be under the other ringleader. The clowns were all scarier looking now and would sneak into the crowd at times and jump scare people.

It was thrilling. The animals were still around, and so were some of the other acts, but Jug had upped the ante so much that there were even times that some of the trainers and other workers of the circus were fearful of their safety. If Jug ever sensed that someone would defect, meals that week would be bountiful with fresh meat.

He wasted no time in setting examples, and in time everyone would fall into line. Those who remained and never questioned Jug's decisions became even more fiercely loyal than they already had been, especially once the results started to show.

The circus continued to move from town to town like it always had under the previous ringleader. While Jug was much more brutal and his reign was filled with terror, thrills, and an iron fist, even he understood the importance of not remaining in one spot for too long. While he wasn't as cautious as his predecessor, he ran a tight ship and trusted those who remained not to be overly careless. Now that everything was up to him, he was running all the shots. The giants were still the guards, and the old lady, somehow still alive and telling fortunes, was always telling him what lied ahead in the future.

She would often whisper to him tales of the future. That it continued to be filled with blood and murder. That the circus would run for years under his rule. That no one would take his place and that the circus would remain under him until his dying days.

When pressured about how he would die, the old lady would never give him a clear picture. She said she could not always see specifics and that often her visions would just come to her when they wanted, but that she was always seeing a woman who would somehow be the end of him. When he pushed her for more, she could only reveal that she had lighter hair and that it would be someone who hunted him down, and then he would hunt her down until it ended in one final violent confrontation.

This angered Jug even further. He didn't know who this woman would be, or when she would come. To avoid it altogether, the giants were ordered to never allow anyone with lighter hair to enter the circus. When this became an obviously difficult task to pull off, the clowns would be dispatched to keep a close eye on them and to make sure that none of them were to ever get anywhere near Jug.

The old lady would also inform Jug about other important visions that she had. That he would need to hire more help, whether a certain person he was going to hire would be a good fit or not, and whether a new idea that he had for an act would really hit it off with the audience and help bring in some extra income.

***

"I have to tell you something," the old lady said as she came walking into Jug's tent after the show ended.

"What is it?" he asked as he looked at her reflection in his vanity mirror, removing his makeup slowly.

"I have seen something that will begin our downfall."

Jug smirked and laughed her off for a second; continuing with the removal of his makeup until she came closer and he could see that she was visibly distraught.

"What is it? What bothers you old woman?"

"A fire, there will be a great fire that burns us to the ground. I can feel the heat on my face, even now as I think back to the vision that I had."

Jug stared at her for a second before turning back to his vanity.

"There will be no fire. Besides, you said that there would be a woman who would be the end of me. What of her? Was she also in this vision that you had?"

The old lady didn't answer as her hands and lips trembled with fear. She stared at Jug for a moment before lowering her head and mumbling something to herself.

"Speak up hag."

"Yes!" she shouted, causing Jug to flinch slightly. "She was the one who set the fire in my vision. Only this time she had a name. I heard it be spoken."

Jug laughed again obviously entertained by the woman's tale of fire and fury.

"Tell me then, what was her name?"

"Shilo Rayne."

Suddenly Jug's laughs came to a stop, and the old lady watched as he slammed his fists onto the top of his vanity. He let out a shout as he punched the mirror, shattering it into dozens of pieces, and then kicked it over with a loud crash.

Suddenly a few clowns came running in along with one of the giants. Jug was standing over his wrecked vanity, panting, obviously enraged, and with his hands on his hips. He began to pace back and forth for a moment before stopping and realizing that others had entered the tent.

"Everything is fine!" he yelled causing them to all quickly disperse.

The old lady continued to stare at him, bewildered and wondering why he reacted in such a way. Even though she knew that her vision was to blame, it was not until she named the girl that Jug had actually become seriously distraught.

"Who is this girl Jug? Do you know her?"

Jug held his hand up as if to signal for her to stop.

After a few seconds passed he picked up his bat and turned to the old lady, half his makeup gone and a sadistic smile crossing his face but his big bulging eyes full of disdain and resentment. He stared at her for a long moment before turning and heading out of the tent and leaving her alone inside.

***

"Gather the fiends," Jug said as he approached the tent area for the clowns, eerie music playing from inside of one of them until the clown Jug just gave an order to went inside and began to shout.

As the music was abruptly shut off, a dozen clowns came out of their tents and began to line up in front of Jug waiting to see what he wanted.

He paced back and forth in front of them as he gently tapped his bat in his opposite hand, stopping only for a moment when another clown came out and joined the rest of the ranks.

"I have a mission for all of you, for all of us," he said as he stopped and turned to look at them all.

"Sure boss, whaddya need?"

"There is a girl. I need her brought to me or killed. Whichever you're capable of doing. I want it done, and I want it done quickly."

"Sounds easy enough," one of the clowns said as he stepped forward from the others. "Point us in a direction, and we will get this done for you."

Jug nodded slightly as one of the giants showed up and stood by his side.

"Need me to tag along boss?" he asked with his deep voice.

Jug thought for a moment as he looked across the faces of all the clowns. He wasn't sure how many to send, and he wasn't sure if he should send one of the giants to go along with them. In doing so, it would leave the security of the circus limited, and he didn't want to have to worry about it, but they were about to pack up and head to the next city soon anyway, so they weren't going to need the extra hands for the time being.

Jug looked around at each of the clowns and hand-picked a few of them, telling the giant to join with them and then dismissing the rest of them. Once they were alone and it was just Jug and his chosen ones, he pointed to the clown with the blue hair in the black and white suit and designated him as the one who would be in charge.

"I have someone I need you all to hunt down for me as I said before. We are leaving this place and will be moving on to our next city. I don't know where she is, I don't know who she's with, and I don't know how you can find her or what she even really looks like."

"So. you want us to hunt someone down, but you don't know where we can find her or what she looks like?" the giant said as he tried to comprehend what Jug was asking them.

"That is exactly what I want you to do."

"Boss, no offense, but how the hell are we supposed to do that?" the clown in the suit inquired as some of the other clowns behind him began to whisper to each other.

"That's for all of you to figure out. I've tasked you with something, and now you have to go out and do it."

Suddenly one of the clowns stepped forward and raised his hand. Everyone turned and looked as Jug stared at him.

"I mean it's kind of stupid, isn't it? Do you even know who she is? Why is she such a problem? Is she really a threat to us?"

Jug continued to stare at the clown for a second before he suddenly thrust a knife into the clown's throat. The clown couldn't even react because of how fast Jug was. He startled gurgling as the blade severed his windpipe and reached up to Jug's hands struggling to pull them away but as he did the blood began to pour out of his throat, and he collapsed to the ground.

Jug knelt and hovered over the clown, looking down into his large eyes as he reached up and gasped for breath. Jug then looked up to the giant and nodded his head once. The giant returned the nod and in one swift motion, he slammed his boot down onto the clown's head and smashed it like he was stepping onto an egg with a loud wet sounding crunch.

Jug let out a giggle before wiping his blade on the dead clown's sleeve. Once his blade was sparkling in the moonlight, he stood up and turned to the other clowns.

"Anyone else?" he asked.

Silence.

"If anyone else has any issues, take care of them," Jug said as he looked over to the giant. "Keep them in line. All of them."

"Yes, sir," the giant returned, turning to look down at the others.

"Now, before we had that interruption. I was going to say that I do have some information for all of you to go off. I don't know if it will help, but it's better than starting with nothing."

"Anything will help," the head clown said.

"I have a name, and I know where she may be staying. Her name is Shilo Rayne, she has blonde hair, and she's in her late teens now I believe."

Jug then went on to describe to the clown's anything else that he could recall from the old lady's vision and then informed them of an address to take a look at and what city it would be in. It was going to be a place they would be eventually passing in their travels, but it was a few states away from where they were now. He repeated the importance of capturing her alive and bringing her to him, but if it was deemed to be an impossibility, to do what needed to be done and to make sure she was dealt with. If she was with anyone else, he wanted them taken care of too. No witnesses, none.

The clowns all agreed and began to gather their things for the trip ahead. Once they were all packed up and ready to go, Jug joined them one last time to stress the importance of their mission. If they returned empty-handed and without proof of their deeds, he would kill all of them.

"We won't fail you, boss," the clown in the suit said. "I do have one question running through my head though."

Jug turned to him as the clown remained and stared at the others as they loaded their things onto a truck.

"What's that?" Jug asked.

"This girl that you're having us go after. I'm just curious to know why she's so important to you. It doesn't matter, I'm just curious is all."

A few seconds of silence passed, causing the clown to look over at Jug who was now no longer looking at him but was facing forward and staring at the truck.

"She's my sister," Jug announced to the clown before he turned around and walked back in the direction of his tent, the clown in the suit staring at Jug in shock until he faded away and disappeared into the shadows.

Part Three

 # Chapter 11

A candle flickers as a shadowy figure inside of a tent rocks back and forth, chanting in a low tone and reaching over to tap a small bell-like gong every so often. The figure continues chanting, slowly waving their arms around in a sweeping motion, and then suddenly all the candles around them extinguished from the gust their quickly passing arms created. As the smoke rises from the candles, the figure leans forward and bows before slowly rising to their feet and lowering their hood, revealing long hair and an aged face.

"So, what did you see fortune teller?" a male voice said coming from behind the woman.

The old woman slowly looked over her shoulder towards the figure standing beyond the wall of beads that hung from the ceiling. She closed her eyes briefly before suddenly opening them and turning to face the figure.

"I saw someone running through trees and bushes, pushing through thorn bushes and falling to the ground only to get up and continue running. She's scared, worried, determined. Something driving her to get away from something, but a part of her longs to return. She's seeking something or someone."

"Hmmph," the person on the other side of the beads grunted. "That's of no use to me. If it weren't for the money you brought in, I'd of let you go a long time ago. At least you're good with fooling people, but your visions are certainly based more on you being senile than psychic."

The old woman turned and approached the beads, looking up to the shadow with strength in her eyes, unafraid of the man.

"Your arrogance is going to be your downfall Jug. Your inability to see things outside of what you perceive as your own version of reality is going to ultimately lead you to your doom."

Suddenly Jug reached through the beads and grabbed the woman by the wrist, squeezing it tightly and pulling her closer, his makeup-covered face coming into view as he leaned into the beads revealing his face with a big grin on it.

"This is my circus, and nobody will take it away from me. I'll destroy it myself if I have to. It ends with me."

The old lady yanked her arm from Jug's grasp and gently rubbed it with her other hand, walking out into the center of her tent and coming to a stop beside a table with a crystal ball on it.

"Perhaps you will get your wish after all," the old woman said as she turned and walked out of her tent into the daylight, Jug remaining inside and shouting obscenities at her until she was out of view.

As the woman took a deep breath and took in the fresh air outside, she could hear glass shatter from the inside of her tent. Without glancing back or worrying about it, she walked away and headed towards the big top tent on the far side of the concourse.

While walking towards the large striped tent that easily towered over all the other tents in the area, most of which were still being put together and lifted, several carnies and clowns would wave to the woman as she walked by.

The woman continued, stopping briefly at a concession stand being constructed before moving onto an area full of tables. She paused again, looking around at the area before she felt a familiar tingle flutter through her body. She immediately looked over to one of the tables to her right and then down to the ground, blinking several times and envisioning a dead body lying there before it disappeared.

She shook her head after dismissing it, continuing to walk towards the big top.

Once there she entered in through the center, watching as the main support beam was being tied down and finally secured, a cheer crossing the ocean of helpers who were putting the tent up as several people stepped away and looked up towards the top.

A gust of wind created a wave that flowed through the fabric of the tent, several animals calling out rambunctiously from an area off to the right side.

The lady took a few more steps into the tent, suddenly stumbling and falling to one knee as she grabbed her head with one hand.

All around her was a fire. Everywhere she looked all she could do was see flames, burning wood, and ash raining down. At the center of the tent was some sort of a scuffle, but all she could do was see the black outlines of two figures against a wall of fire on the other side of them.

Just as quickly as the fiery vision came, it was gone. When the woman came to and recollected herself, several people were standing around and inquiring if she was okay. She reassured them that she was, and then with aid, rose back up. She thanked those who showed concern and then walked in the direction of where the animals were, concealing her true emotions until she was alone with the animals on the other side of a wall aligned with bleachers.

She began to breathe quickly as she tried to make the visions go away, but even now while looking around at the animals, she could see them springing forth from their cages and running around in such chaos that the woman could not comprehend what she was really looking at. She then rushed outside beginning to gag and cough, feeling her eyes water and sting.

A few seconds and deep breathes later, and she was okay again, the visions now gone.

They always came in waves. She could meditate and

focus and try to force one to happen, but it wasn't always a guarantee that one would. Sometimes her meditations would open doors a little too much. They would not just allow her to see one thing, but instead, she would become haunted and flooded with visions for an extended period until they would finally subside. That was exactly what she was experiencing now, and no matter how used to it she thought she would become, especially with dozens of years of experiences, it always took its toll on her and made her exhausted.

The visions weren't always clear or make sense either. Sometimes they seemed to be subjective depending on the choices one would make, while other times they seemed clear and precise and definite like nothing could alter the course of what would be coming. It was up to her to differentiate and try to interpret what she could see.

She then thought of Jug and his arrogance. She was sure that what she was experiencing was going to be the path ahead unless he changed his ways, but she was tired of trying to give him warnings that he would only dismiss yet would always return to ask for something more.

It wasn't her duty to tell people what to change. She learned that from her mother who also had the gift. She told her from a young age that the gift came to those who entrusted it, but who did not interfere. Tell others and share what you saw, but don't get directly involved or try to alter or manipulate future events. That would only lead to greed or certain doom, and her mother warned her that sometimes the actual act of trying to alter choices and behaviors is what ultimately caused the predictions to come true to begin with. It was a tricky and tiring gift to have that came with great responsibility, but if used for the right reasons, it could be controlled and used for great things.

The old woman chose to be neutral when it came to what she saw. While she did use her gift to try and make a living so that she could survive, she was always a drifter until she joined the circus at a young age. She thought back to those days, long before Jug was a thorn in her side and tried to abuse her gifts for his own personal gains and before he was even born. She remembered when she used to get excited about seeing the futures of people and telling them of happy days to come. Tales of marriage, children, houses, and family gatherings used to be the majority of what she saw. Somewhere along the way, however, the world seemed to become a much darker place. The happy visions slowly began to come further and further apart, and instead, were now replaced by selfish desires, jealous lovers, anxiety-ridden worries, and the fears of people worried about things out of their control.

It was a shame, and she wished it was how it used to be, but she knew that the world had changed. There was no going back, at least not anymore. Instead, the world was only going to continue to get worse until it ended, or something drastic occurred to shift the way society and those within it saw the world and those around them.

The old woman walked around outside of the big top tent for several more minutes before noticing Jug walk inside of it not noticing her as he entered. She waited a second until she could hear him beginning to cheer and clap that the tent was put up, and then walked past the entrance and headed off to return to her own tent.

She thought about how far they had come from Jug's predecessor. From the old days of just trying to create entertainment like all the other circuses, to now creating something that was beyond exhilarating and always stunned the crowd but had a cost for those who stuck around or were too interested in seeing more.

Suddenly one of the two giants of the circus walked by, and the old woman glanced up at him. He stopped as if he wanted to say something, but then lowered his head and continued towards the big top. The old woman continued on her way back knowing exactly what the giant had been thinking. She could tell from his eyes that he knew Jug was out of control. Especially with now having sent out a bunch of his clowns and the other giant to go and find the girl named Shilo from her vision.

Sadly, there was nothing that any of them could do, and leaving was not an option. Jug would find a way to track you down. If he didn't have you killed for desertion where he found you, then you would just be brought back for dinner. Whether for the clowns, himself, or the animals.

When the old lady finally arrived back at her tent, she was slow to enter. She knew she was going to walk into a mess, and as she entered inside, she wasn't surprised by what she saw. The table with the crystal ball that had been on it was flipped over. The beads on the opposite wall torn down, some strands broken, and beads scattered randomly across the floor. Shelves were torn down, and random jars that she had full of herbs on them had been shattered, the glass littering the area.

The old woman continued in, stepping on the glass as she began to look around. It only took her a few seconds to find the old brown cloth that had kept the crystal ball covered from Jug's rampage. It had rolled into the corner of the room, and upon further inspection, the crystal ball was not cracked or damaged in any way.

Letting out a sigh of relief, the woman turned the table back over and returned the ball to its proper resting place atop it. Then, without hesitation, the woman began to clean up the mess just like all the other times that she had to clean up after Jug. He would never truly harm her, but he took twisted pleasure in making her life miserable sometimes, especially when he didn't get his way or the answers he was hoping for. As much as he didn't want to admit it, at the end of the day, he needed her. The old woman knew, however, that as much as she thought she knew Jug, he was at times unpredictable and you could never truly know how he was going to react or what he was going to do next.

 # Chapter 12

The old woman tossed and turned in her bed, restless and disturbed by her dreams. She moaned, rolling back and forth in her cot until she went off the side and awoke as she **hit the ground.** She stayed there for a minute, shaking and dazed by her traumatic dream experience.

Sometimes the visions came at night when she slept. It was only then that she could not regain control until she was awake. In her sleep, they were at their most potent. Visually powerful, full of emotions, and raw. She could experience them as if she were there, rather than like a passing ghost or déjà vu like memory during the day. Sometimes they were precognitive, and she could envision the future. At other times, they were flashbacks to the past, whether her own or of ancestors long before.

This one was of the future. Her future. She foresaw the flames like she had the day before, only this time it was accompanied by flashes of lights and sounds of thunder. A sense of falling overcame her, but she could not recall if it was from the vision, or her actually falling from the bed and hitting the floor where she still was lying. Her chest did hurt, and when she reached and pressed on it, it was tender.

After staying on the floor, the old woman eventually got up, taking her time and then heading outside for some fresh air.

The moon was out and high in the sky. The stars accompanying it were countless, and as soon as the old woman turned around, she saw a shooting star streak across the sky above the big top, its tail leaving a residue that was quick to fade away.

Just then there was a loud honk from a vehicle over by the gates to the circus. The old lady turned and could see the beams of light from the headlights as the shapes of people walking around passed in front of them. Curious, she began to head over in the vehicle's direction. By the time she had gotten there, the gate had already been opened, and two trucks had pulled in and were parked just inside. One of the clowns closed the gate as several others got out of the vehicles.

That was when the old woman recognized the clowns as the ones that Jug had sent out days before to spread the flyers for the circus arriving near town.

"Hey, grandma," one of the clowns said jokingly acknowledging her presence as he walked towards the back of the truck.

Some of the other clowns laughed while others paid no attention and began to unload several large crates from the back of the other truck. As they brought them down, the old woman could start to hear mumbles coming from the truck where the one clown had disappeared behind. The mumbles continued until suddenly a girl came into view, being dragged by the clown along the ground, her hands, and feet bound by rope. Almost just as quickly as she screamed, one of the other clowns jumped in and punched her in the face, knocking her out instantly. The clown who had been dragging her then picked her up and threw her over his shoulder, walking away from the truck and out towards the tents and giving the old woman a dirty look as he passed.

"I thought you were supposed to be spreading the word of the circus? Don't you think taking a townie and bringing her here is going to be suspicious? That a local's gone missing the same time we show up?" the old woman said to one of the clowns still unloading crates from the truck.

He stopped for a moment and put his hands on his hips as he took a breath.

"We know Jug doesn't want any unnecessary attention. We usually don't pick anyone up until the day of or night before we leave. This way by the time anyone notices someone is gone, we're already nowhere to be found. This girl isn't a local or a townie though."

"So, who is she then?" the old woman persisted.

"A drifter. We found her walking along the highway."

"Towards the town or away from it?"

"I don't remember, and I don't have time for this old woman. If you want answers go find them out yourself," the clown said, returning his attention to the truck and crates.

The old woman watched him for a moment more before turning around and walking away, headed off in the direction that she saw the girl being carried. Several minutes later she found her inside a tent with the clown who had taken her away. He turned around and stared at her as she approached the entrance to the tent, the girl's clothes already stripped from her body, and gave her a dirty look, closing the front of the large tent and disappearing out of view.

The woman stayed by the tent before placing her hand on it. She closed her eyes and could feel the fear and terror emanating from the still unconscious woman. As the clown could be heard grunting inside, and the creaking of a table wiggling back and forth, the old woman took a seat on the chair beside her just outside and waited for the clown to be done. Once he let out a pleasurable moan, he exited the tent and paused, looking down to the woman before smiling and headed off towards the big top. Once he was out of view, the old woman slowly stood up, entered the tent, and then walked over to the girl.

She was lying on the wooden table naked. Her eyes were open, staring up at the ceiling of the tent, but she wasn't responsive and was in a catatonic state, not even glancing over at the old lady as she approached. Upon further inspection, her body had bruises and cuts all over it that the old woman didn't notice earlier because she was clothed. Some were fresher than others.

The old woman leaned over her and peered into her widened fear-filled eyes. After a second, she then looked around for the girl's clothes, finding them ripped but still together in a messy pile on the floor. She picked them up and began to dress the woman, making sure she was gentle as to not cause any more harm to her and once she was done, she sat in the chair nearby.

A few minutes passed before the girl began to move, glancing over at the old woman and then freezing again in fear.

"Shh, shh," the old woman said in an attempt to comfort, standing up and then gently reaching forward to stroke the girl's hair.

The girl didn't know how to react. She had just been kidnapped by a bunch of crazy clowns and had now just awoken to an old woman who was now standing over her in a tent. All she could do was stare at her for a few seconds before she began to mutter something incoherently.

"What is it?" the old woman inquired, hoping the girl could compose herself and find the words to what she was trying to express.

"Wh-wh-where am I?" she finally asked, pushing the old woman's hands aside as she looked around the tent.

The old woman didn't know how to respond. Sure,

they were at the circus, but that was only going to send the girl into a panic, and she did not want to do that. She could say that she was safe, but she knew that was a lie and the furthest thing possible from the truth.

"What's happened to me? Who are you? What are you going to do to me?"

The girl began to ask questions before the old woman had a chance to answer any of them. Seconds later and she pushed the old woman aside, causing her to fall to the ground before she jumped up and then ran for the tent's exit. Just as she passed through and entered outside, the old woman could see a giant fist swing by and strike the girl in the side of the head, causing her body to go limp and fall to the ground.

The old woman got up and walked outside, the giant that remained at the circus having intercepted the girl and knocked her out.

"I could hear her," he said. "What should I do with her?" he inquired, asking the old woman as she stood over the girl and looked down at her.

"Take her to my tent and tie her down in the back. Don't tell Jug either," she said as the giant nodded, picked the girl up, and then threw her over his shoulder with ease. He then followed the old woman as she led the way back to her tent.

After they got there, the giant brought her in the back. Once he was gone, he inquired what the old woman was going to do with her, but she dismissed him and said she was just going to keep her safe from the clowns.

None of the clowns would dare enter her tent without her permission. While most of them didn't like her, and some dismissed and treated her like a nuisance, others were afraid of her and stayed away. They were scared because of her mystical powers and ability to foresee things. Only Jug would enter her tent without permission, often at times without her even knowing except for the mess that he would leave behind.

The old woman went into the back of her tent, passing through the beaded wall and then stopping beside the still unconscious woman who the giant had tied down for her. She began to gather candles, herbs, and other various items that she would need for a ritual that she had never done before but knew well having seen her mother do it once at a young age. After all the ingredients were accounted for, she lit the candles, prepared herself, and then began to chant in a low tone.

She began to rub the woman's body with a sponge, cleansing it with water that she sprinkled several herbs in. As she did this, the woman started to move slightly, but she was still not awake. She then took a long stem of a plant and held it up to a candle, igniting the end of it and then waving it in a circular motion above the woman, the smoke coming from it filling the room.

The old woman's chanting began to increase in repetition, mumbling words of an incoherent old language that most would never surely ever recognize. As the chanting started to speed up, and the old woman placed the stem of the plant in the water to extinguish it, then mixing several herbs in and then picking up a small knife. She then looked down at the girl, who was now beginning to moan as she was starting to wake up. She took the small knife and cut her own hand, allowing several of the drops to drip into the water, taking the girl's hand and making a small prick in one of her fingers, allowing drops of her blood to enter the water as well.

The girl then opened her eyes, looking around confused and beginning to struggle as she released that she was tied down and couldn't move. She looked over at the old woman who was chanting and now drinking some of the water that she had been infusing with both of their blood and the herbs. She then brought the bowl and leaned over the girl, holding her nose so that she opened her mouth, screaming and then gurgling as the foul-smelling liquid poured into her mouth. The old woman then held the girl's mouth closed, whispering to her that it would help her while the girl resisted, trying to spit out the liquid but unable to, instead coughing and choking on it because she was unable to breathe. When she could not hold on any longer, she gave in, swallowing it and then feeling a warming sensation come over her body as the old woman let go of her mouth and stepped away, the girl entering into another fit of uncontrollable coughing as she fought for air.

The old woman began to laugh, clasping her hands

together and rotating in circles as she chanted and gave praise to some invisible entity or whatever it was that she believed in. The girl on the table was still coughing but was now slowly regaining composure as she watched in horror and unsure of what to do.

Suddenly the old woman stopped moving and chanting with her arms at her side. Now she was standing perfectly still with her back to the girl. After a few seconds, she began to slowly turn around, the candlelight reflecting off her face as it revealed a sinister expression. There was a big grin crossing the old woman's face, and her eyes were large, unblinking, and black.

The girl went to scream, but nothing came out, her voice suppressed by some unseen force. She continued to yell as the old woman slowly approached with her hands and head twitching randomly until she was standing over her. The old woman grabbed her head, holding it while forcing her eyes open as she leaned in and stared down into them. The girl suddenly stopped trying to scream, and instead looked into the old woman's eyes and felt herself being pulled into the darkness she was looking into until her own eyes rolled into the back of her head and everything faded to black.

***

The old woman exited the tent, searching for the giant until she found him sitting in the area of tables near the concession stands. When she approached, he quickly rose to his feet. She then asked if he could retrieve the girl from her tent and bring her back to the clowns with her.

After getting the girl and heading back to the tents where the clowns stayed, they looked at her oddly and wondered why she would return her.

"She's going to be of some use to us," the old woman said. "Until then, do to her as you please."

One of the clowns stepped out from his bunk and approached, looking at the girl whose eyes were open, but it was apparent that she wasn't there and like she was in a coma.

"What kind of spell did you cast on someone now old woman?" he inquired, taking the girl from the giant's arms and lowering her to the ground.

"I put a little part of her inside of me, and a little bit of me inside of her. I foresaw the possibility of betrayal in her future. In doing the ritual I have performed, I can tap into what she can see and feel and manipulate her if need be. She can do so to me as well, although she is not trained in these sorts of gifts, so it is unlikely she will even know I am there within her mind."

"Mind control?" the clown said, looking back to the others and laughing hysterically.

"Not exactly," the old woman replied, a hint of frustration in her voice. "I can't control her. I can only suggest an emotion or thought. It's up to her to act on it."

"That's some freaky shit!" one of the clowns said in the back of the tent.

The clown looked back and forth between the old woman and the girl, the other clowns still laughing at the other clowns' comment.

"Just be warned. Do not kill her. Her death would result in me losing a part of myself. We are linked now."

The clown then pulled out a knife, a smile crossing his face as he brought it to the girl's throat, pressing against it but not hard enough to cause injury.

"Maybe I should do her in and this way we can all be rid of you?" he said while the other clowns all stopped laughing and a few stepped out to see what would happen next.

"Jug would have your head on a platter if harm came to me. Do as you want to her but keep her alive."

The clown stared up at the old woman, tightly squeezing the girl's hair as if about to drive the knife into her throat but after a second, he stopped and let go, sighing in frustration at the old woman's words and knowing that she was right about Jug. His hands were tied.

The old woman smirked while turning and walking away as the clowns approached the girl and dragged her inside, the sounds of grunts and moans echoing until the tent was now far behind her.

She continued to walk, heading back to her tent while the giant followed, clearing his throat as if he wanted to say something.

"Yes?" the old woman said, the giant then scratching the back of his head before finally opening his mouth and speaking.

"What would happen to you?" he asked.

"If she died?"

The giant grunted.

"I would descend into a maddened feral state of existence," she explained. "A risk I'm willing to take if it means I can stop the doom I saw headed our way in the future."

"Why do this?" he asked.

"Because," the old woman said as she came to a stop outside her tent and turned back to the giant. "Jug cannot do this on his own. While I despise him at times, I've also helped raise him like he was my own. I've seen him go from a runaway to the leader of our band of misfits. In some strange way, while I know he grows increasingly tired of me, I do care for him somehow, however, he won't listen to my warnings anymore so more desperate measures must be taken. Maybe in risking myself, I can somehow save this circus."

The giant nodded signifying that he understood what the old woman was saying.

The circus was all she really knew. As much as she was a part of it, it was also that much a part of her. She could not, with a clear conscience, just sit by and let it end, especially after foreseeing how it may happen. In some way she held herself responsible like she was the only one who could prevent it from ending since Jug wouldn't heed her warnings and so even if it meant losing herself in the process, she was ready to do whatever it was going to take to make sure that the show goes on.

Part Four

 # Chapter 13

"So, Shilo, you're sure that you're going to be okay with the house all to yourself?"

"Yes, Mom," Shilo reassured. "You guys are only going to be gone for a week and a half anyway. I'm pretty sure I can manage this all on my own for at least that long."

"Just remember, no parties," a male voice said as it entered the room.

"Dad, with what friends?"

"I know, I'm only kidding," he said as he came over and kissed Shilo on the head. "And you have friends. You just prefer to stay inside than to go outside. Nothing wrong with that, but you do need some fresh air occasionally."

Shilo rolled her eyes as her mom grabbed her coat and then began to roll a large piece of luggage down the hallway towards the front door.

"Remember, if you need to reach us in an emergency, you can call the resort. We will take the first flight back if we need to. Food is in the fridge and if you want to order out at all, just use the card we gave you."

"Everything will be fine you two. You need to go, or

you're going to be late and miss your plane!" Shilo rushed as she began to move her hands into a shooing motion.

After everyone shared a hug and Shilo's parents both walked out of the front door and towards their taxi, they waved at one another before Shilo closed the door. As soon as she clicked the lock and turned around, she leaned back into the door and slowly slid down to the floor with a large exhale of relief.

"Oh, thank god," she said aloud.

Shilo remained sitting with her back against the door until she heard the taxi beep and drive away. A few seconds later she smiled and jumped up to her feet and ran throughout the house cheering. She ran from room to room, both up and down the stairs before flinging open her bedroom door and diving onto her bed.

"Oh, this is going to be great. Finally, some peace and quiet, and the house all to myself!" she shouted in glee as she sat up in her bed and looked out of her window. "But what the fuck am I going to do with myself over the next week and a half?"

Shilo continued to sit on her bed for several minutes before she got up and headed down into the kitchen. First, she checked the pantry, then the cabinets, and lastly the fridge to see what foods her parents went and stocked up on for her. There was more than enough, and an abundant amount of canned goods and food products with expiration dates a long way away. There wasn't anything that jumped out beyond the basic stuff that she usually ate or that her parents would typically cook.

Once done rummaging through the fridge, Shilo turned around with her hands on her hip and stared out across the open kitchen into the living room. Suddenly, Shilo's eyes locked onto the card her parents left for her to use in case she needed to order or buy anything while they were away.

"I know what I'm going to do," Shilo said as she ran across the kitchen and slid on her socks into the living room before diving onto the couch and reaching over to the card. As she flipped it back and forth in between her hands a smile crossed her face, and she raised her arms in victory as she let out a shout.

"Pizza night!" she yelled.

Suddenly a loud bang came from the front of the house and startled Shilo. She looked over her shoulder in the direction of the front door and ducked below the top of the couch to stay out of sight.

A minute passed before she gained the courage to get up and investigate.

Slowly making her way across the living room, then the dining room, and then out into the main foyer with the stairs, she noticed that there was now a pile of letters and mail on the floor that had been slid through the slot on the front door.

Shilo let out a sigh of relief before she laughed at herself for how scared she had got over nothing.

"Real nice Shilo, really nice," she said to herself as she

went and picked the mail up and brought it to the kitchen and then placed it on the table. "Home alone for not even an hour and you already got freaked out over nothing."

After looking through the mail to see if anything were hers, Shilo ran back up to her room and opened her laptop, pulling up the delivery website for the closest pizza place, Dough Oh's, and then began to scour the website so she could place her order.

She quickly began to drop things into her order's shopping cart. From two medium-sized pizzas with different toppings, the first being ham and onions, the second being broccoli and chicken, to an order of boneless wings and one of their double chocolate brownies for dessert. Her mouth was salivating just thinking about the food, and as she checked out and placed the order, she quickly ran back downstairs and began the painfully long wait for the food to show up.

***

About half an hour passed before Shilo saw the headlights from a car travel across the wall above the tv she was watching. She rolled over onto her belly and stared out of the dining room window across the way, listening anxiously and hoping that it was her food. A few seconds later a car door was slammed shut, and she could hear someone walking up onto the wooden deck in the front of the house.

Then the doorbell rang.

Shilo jumped up so quickly she slipped on the wooden floor and fell back onto the couch. The second time she jumped up she did it much more carefully and then headed as quick as she could towards the front door with a laugh.

"I'm coming!" she shouted as the doorbell rang once again.

Shilo pulled the front door open so fast that it startled the pizza delivery kid on the other side. The boy looked at Shilo for a second before his eyes traveled to the massive interior of the house behind her.

As his eyes grew big in astonishment, Shilo cleared her throat. A brief second later and the delivery boy snapped out of the mesmerized state that he was in and looked at her, bewildered. He shook his head and then slid the pizzas and other food out of his bag, before handing everything to Shilo.

"Thank you," Shilo replied as all she could think about was the food.

Shilo then gave the boy a tip, and he slowly began to walk away as he continued to stare at the house while Shilo closed the front door.

Everyone always had the same reaction when they first looked inside of her and her parent's house. Whenever the door opened, it was always at that same moment that awe-filled their eyes and their brains tried to comprehend everything that they could see. It was not a mansion, but Shilo's parents had money, and they used it calculatingly over the years, meticulously planning and making sure that the interior design was both high-quality, and exceptionally well taken care of.

"Oh my god, finally," Shilo shouted out with glee as she practically sprinted into the kitchen with her food and placed it carefully on top of the counter at the end of the peninsula.

She then flipped the pizza box open, and as the smell hit her nose and her eyes gazed at the pizza, she could begin to feel her mouth salivate even more now.

"It looks so fucking good. Ah!"

Shilo didn't even bother to get any plates. She didn't want to do any dishes after and decided that eating straight out of the box was going to be the easiest thing to do. All she wanted to do was relax, eat food, and be carefree while her parents were away. It was just her now, and she was going to make the absolute best of it and enjoy it as much as she possibly could.

Once Shilo was done examining all the food and making sure that she had everything, she got herself a drink of soda and then plopped herself on the couch and turned on the big television. She surfed the channels and came to a stop at a horror movie about some house on a hill with a young girl as the main character before turning to another channel that had some girl in a big dress walking around some big creepy-looking mansion. Shilo continued to watch it for a few minutes until she found out the mansion was haunted, and she decided that was enough for her.

She wasn't thrilled with horror movies unless it was near Halloween. She was all about action movies and crime shows, especially the ones where the bad guy always got caught in the end, so she looked for a show like that and came to a stop once she was able to finally find one.

"Ugh this food is so good," Shilo said in between bites of a slice of pizza as she pulled the cheese off another and dangled it above her head before slowly lowering it into her mouth.

By the time the show she was watching came to an end, Shilo had nearly finished one entire pizza, her wings, and one slice of the second pizza.

"I don't want to wait to eat you, but I know exactly what I'm going to use you both for tomorrow," Shilo said to the remaining slices of pizza and her untouched brownie. "I'm going to be eating both of you for breakfast!"

Shilo cheered in jubilation for a few seconds, her voice bouncing off the walls and high ceiling as it echoed throughout the house. For a moment she covered her mouth but was quick to remember that her parents weren't home and that she was alone. She then giggled before taking the remaining food and putting it into the refrigerator.

Seconds later the phone rang and caused Shilo to jump.

"Shit!" she shouted as the phone rang once more before she picked it up.

"He-hello?" she inquired.

"Hi dear, it's Mom! How is everything?"

"Hi Mom, everything is fine. I just got done eating some food. How was your flight?"

"It was great! Dad didn't enjoy the turbulence and got a little ill, but now we're just getting settled into our room at the resort and just wanted to check in with you."

"Everything is good here on my end," Shilo comforted. "It's weird being in the house all alone, but I've got it handled."

"I know you'll be fine Hun. Anyway, your father says hello and is making faces at me to leave you be. He wants to go downstairs and stuff his face, as usual-"

"As usual," Shilo said at the same time as her mother. They both shared a laugh.

"Well, just make smart choices as they say. I'll call back in a few days to check in on you. Love you, sweetheart," Shilo's mom said as her dad could be heard saying it further away on the other end of the line.

"Love you guys too. Have fun!"

A second later Shilo's mom hung up, and Shilo let out a big yawn as she stretched her arms outward before placing the phone back on the wall.

"Fuck that food wore me out," she said to the empty kitchen.

Shilo returned to the couch to continue watching her show, yawning once again, but before she knew it, she was drifting asleep and couldn't fight it off any longer.

 # Chapter 14

Shilo woke up a few hours later. It was not quite the morning yet, and the sun was not up, but she was still in the same position on the couch with the television still on.

"Holy crap," she said to herself as she sat up and looked around bewildered and in disbelief that she slept through the television blaring and all the lights still on.

Shilo hit the power button on the tv's remote and then turned all the lights off before ascending the stairs back to her room. After climbing in her bed, she pulled the covers over herself and stared out of her window until she drifted asleep again.

***

The next morning the sun rose, and its light shone through Shilo's window and hit her right in the face. She flinched and woke up, pulling one of her pillows onto her head to resist the coming of a new day, but to no avail.

The birds outside were chirping, and cars drove by the house. After a few minutes of continuing to hide beneath her pillow, she became frustrated and heaved it across the room, sitting up and letting out a disgust-filled moan.

"What am I going to do with myself today?" she asked herself out loud as she pondered about the possibilities of the day.

She sat idly in her bed for a few minutes, looking across her room, then out of the window, and then turning to her door and listening to the silence coming from the other side. Another minute passed before she slowly got out of bed and headed to the bathroom to do her morning routines.

"Pizza for breakfast!" she shouted in glee after opening the refrigerator and seeing the pizza staring back at her. "But do I want you cold or to heat you up?" she asked the food. "Hmm, cold it is."

Shilo relished in the leftovers, heating her brownie after but exploding it in the microwave for having it in for too long.

"Goddamnit," she murmured having to now clean it up.

Once she was done, she went upstairs and got dressed, still unsure what she was going to be doing for the day, but she knew that leaving the house was a must.

By the time she was closing the front door and standing in the yard Shilo had decided that she was going to go to the mall. As she walked towards the car, she stopped and stared out as several cars passed, noticing that there was an odd-looking van parked on the side of the road a few houses down that she did not ever remember seeing before. She stared at it for a minute before it suddenly turned around, cutting into traffic and almost hitting a car in the process before taking off in the opposite direction.

"Huh. I wonder what that was about?" she asked herself before shaking it off as nothing and getting in her parent's car.

Shilo spent the entire ride to the mall wondering what she was going to be doing once she got there. She had just eaten breakfast, so stopping to get more Dough Oh's was surely both unhealthy and unnecessary. To justify it, she thought if she were at the mall all day and could walk off the calories that she could get it for lunch, or better yet, dinner again, but she dismissed the idea.

Once at the mall and finally inside, Shilo walked around aimlessly for hours. In and out of stores, some of her favorites and some she had never bothered to go into before. She had no sense of purpose being there. She wasn't looking for anything specific, and she wasn't trying to accomplish anything other than to kill some time. She didn't want to be inside of her house for the entirety of her parents being away, but she also wanted to be able to say that she at least got out once and could have been seen in public.

Once boredom began to take over, Shilo left the mall and decided to drive around a while. She went through downtown, slowing down and peering at the storefronts in between the people walking by before driving out towards the outlets where everything was at a discounted price. She was tempted to pull in and go shopping, but as she was approaching the entrance, there was a familiar-looking sight. Following a few cars behind her, Shilo thought that she saw the same van that was parked outside her home and a few houses down.

Shilo drove past the outlets, continuing onto the highway and keeping an eye on her rearview mirror. When the two cars behind her both turned into the outlets, and the third changed lanes and sped off on her right and exited, the van was now the only vehicle remaining that was directly behind her. She studied it, trying to see if she could get a glimpse of the driver, but the windshield was too dirty. She could make out that two people were sitting up front, but she couldn't see their faces or any other details. The van was beaten up and covered in rust, with dents and one of the headlights missing. Besides that, and the missing front license plate, Shilo couldn't get anything else from the odd vehicle that she was convinced was following her for some reason.

"C'mon you fuckers. I dare you to keep following me!" she shouted in her car as the van suddenly sped up and changed lanes.

Shilo's heart was racing as the van continued to speed up, quickly approaching the side of her vehicle and then slowing down as it came alongside it. Shilo looked over and tried to see up through the driver's side window, but it too was dirty to the point of not being able to see through it. Every time Shilo went to speed up or slow down, the van matched her speed, and now she was really beginning to get concerned.

Out of frustration she leaned over and stuck her middle finger up, hoping that whoever was in the van would look over and see it.

A second later the van sped up faster than Shilo and quickly exited the highway off to the right as she continued forward.

"What the fuck was that all about?" she asked herself as she doubled checked her rearview mirror a dozen more times for any trace of the van's return.

After she was sure that she was no longer being followed, and too creeped out to stay out in public to do anything else, she headed home. As Shilo pulled into the driveway, she sat in the car for a few more minutes. She leaned back in her seat and looked both ways down the street as best as she could. She wanted to make sure that the van wasn't parked anywhere nearby, and after seeing that it was clear, Shilo got out of the car and sprinted inside of the house.

Once in, she slammed the door behind her, locked it, and then sighed in relief.

"Thank fucking god." She mumbled before placing the keys on the counter in the kitchen and heading into the pantry for some much-needed stress eating.

Shilo checked every corner of the pantry and grabbed something from each section. Chips, cookies, carrot sticks, peanut butter, cheese, and a big bag of popcorn. She returned to the microwave, sticking the popcorn inside and starting it while she began to prepare the rest of her food. After everything was ready, she ran up to her room and stayed hidden there, stuffing her face with everything until she was full and fell backward into her pillows in a food coma.

A minute later and she started giggling at what happened and how she was now laying on her bed and surrounded by empty bags, crumbs, and a half-eaten jar of peanut butter.

Her stomach then grumbled because of how much she ate, and she laughed again.

The rest of the day Shilo stayed in her room. She watched shows on the television on her desk until the sun went down. Eventually, she heard a familiar bang downstairs, but she knew that it was the mail. A few minutes later she went down and got it, going through it and looking for anything of importance.

There was a letter addressed to her from the state college.

Shilo pulled the letter out and quickly opened it, standing in the center of the kitchen as she read it out loud to herself, soon discovering that she was accepted for the nursing program and that she could start the following year as a freshman.

"Yes!" she shouted as she jumped up and down in the

kitchen before running around the house waving the letter wildly in the air in celebration. "I can't wait to tell mom and dad!" she said as she stared at the phone on the kitchen wall.

She wanted to call them right away to tell them, but they were on vacation and Shilo didn't want to ruin it by having them thinking about that the entire time. She thought it would be better to wait once they were home so rather than post-vacation blues, they could have something else to be excited about.

***

Two more days passed.

Shilo didn't leave the house once. She stayed inside watching movies, television show marathons, and gorging herself on food in solitary celebration. She almost let the college acceptance news slip when she talked to her parents on the phone while they updated her on how everything was going on their end. Luckily, she caught herself and instead changed the subject, telling her mom about how she went out to the mall but avoided mentioning the crazy van on the road so her mother didn't worry or give her a lecture about driving safely.

They then discussed some of the activities and adventures they had been on. They went out on a big boat and went scuba diving, where Shilo's dad didn't want to get out of the water and was having an immense amount of fun. Her mom said they also checked out an ancient stone temple from thousands of years ago and even went spelunking in a massive cave.

Shilo continued to talk with her mom for a few more minutes before they both said goodbye and hung up the phones, her mom saying that she would call again a day or two before they were leaving to check in one last time.

She was happy that it sounded like her parents were having a blast. That was the whole point of the trip anyway. Meanwhile, Shilo was enjoying having the house to herself. While it was odd and she missed not having her mother playing music and having it traveling through the house or hearing her father in the kitchen cooking or singing along, it was so peaceful.

Then she thought about college and what kind of chaos that was going to be bringing into her life. She longed to have something to do, and she always liked being intellectually challenged, but doing the homework and studying was not going to be something she was looking forward to. Being a nurse, however, was a dream of hers.

Shilo loved to help people. While her parents were both business people, she was on the more compassionate side of career choices.

Suddenly there was a knocking sound, and Shilo quickly turned to stare at the front door, wondering if maybe something was supposed to be coming and getting delivered.

She looked through the window on the side of the door and noticed a big brown vehicle outside and someone standing out front holding a big package, so she quickly opened the door up and greeted the man. She then signed a piece of paper he had and took the package, standing in the front yard and looking down at it as he drove away.

Shilo gently shook the box, curious about what was inside as she turned the box over in her hands and read the label that was on it.

It was the wrong address.

"Shit!" Shilo said, quickly running across her front yard and waving to the truck that was now too far down the road to notice her.

She didn't know whose package it was. The address was only a few houses down, however, so Shilo made it her mission to make the delivery herself.

After running inside to get her shoes, she walked on the sidewalk with the package and delivered it to the correct house, leaving it on the front steps after nobody responded to the doorbell or her knocking.

On the way back Shilo was admiring the beautiful weather and took a few deep breaths in, smelling one of her neighbor's flower bushes by the fence along the way.

Just then a strange-sounding vehicle engine could be heard far off behind her.

Shilo turned to see what kind of car or truck it was

coming from but instead noticed an all too familiar vehicle now parked on the side of the road a few houses further down than the one she had delivered the package to.

It was the rusty van that she had encountered on the highway.

"What the fuck," she said to herself suddenly feeling the hair on her arms stand up.

The van sat there as Shilo stared at it, slowly beginning to walk back towards her house. After a few steps, the van suddenly started to move, slowly, in her direction.

Shilo quickly turned around and began to walk faster to her house, glancing over her shoulder at the van as it continued towards her and began to speed up. A second later she found herself running now and practically in a full sprint across her front yard as the van quickly accelerated down the street.

As she fumbled with the keys to open the front door, she repeatedly shouted obscenities under her breath until she finally got in and slammed the door behind her, locking it and then peeking out of the window and watching as the van sped by and disappeared out of view.

 # Chapter 15

"Whew," she said, freaked out once again by the same dirty, rusty van that she keeps seeing.

It was a few days since she got into an altercation with them on the road. She wondered who they were and what they wanted. Maybe they were just kids being a bunch of assholes in the first vehicle they could afford to get off the side of some road. Or, perhaps, it was some lunatic that had their eyes on her or was trying to rob the house since it was one of the nicest houses on the block.

Whatever the case was, Shilo knew that she would be safe indoors and was determined not to leave the house again until her parents were home, figuring that whoever the freak or freaks were, they'd probably be gone by then and moved onto someone else to stalk or creep out. After all, she had more than enough food in the pantry and had no reason to go outside unless another package got accidentally delivered, and even then, she would leave it outside and wasn't tempted to step foot out her front door no matter what the reason would be.

After pacing back and forth for a few minutes, she

walked around and made sure that all the doors and windows were locked just in case. Once that was accomplished, she felt relief after peering outside and seeing that there was no sign of the strange vehicle anywhere.

"Okay, Shilo. Time to get your mind off things and to entertain yourself," she said as she walked into the kitchen and stared out across the living room.

A few seconds later she found herself in the pantry again, gathering a bunch of items to cook a small dinner. After dinner, she gathered up a bunch of snacks and returned to her room upstairs, excited to start a new show on television that she saw a new season had come out for.

***

Shilo woke up to screaming. Panicking, she jumped up in bed only to notice that it was coming from her television and that she had fallen asleep while watching. When she rolled over and looked at the clock on her nightstand, she saw that it was the middle of the night. She then turned the television off and cleaned up the mess she had on her bed before heading downstairs to get a glass of water.

She slowly descended the stairs, pausing briefly to stare out across the empty dark house and watching as a beam of light passed through the windows from a passing car. She then headed into the kitchen, poured a glass of water, and stood beside the peninsula taking sips and just thinking about her future, being accepted into college, and everything that she had gone through to get this far.

Shilo then made eye contact, briefly, with a family portrait on the far side of the living room that was sitting on top of a shelf.

Suddenly she thought she saw movement at the corner of her eye. Half-heartedly taking a glance over towards the front door, a shadow moved past the window on the side. Shilo stared at the window for a moment, waiting to see what it was, but nothing happened, and so she dismissed it, thinking that she imagined it because of still being in a state of half-awareness.

Shilo then turned to place the glass in the sink. As she did, she thought she saw movement by the front door again, only this time it was accompanied by a light thud.

When she looked over, she froze by what she was looking at.

Someone was looking in through the window.

There was a face with two hands above the eyes pressed up against the glass of the window beside the front door. It looked like whoever it was, was studying the inside of the house and searching for something, or someone.

That was when Shilo realized what the person looking in the window looked like.

It was a clown.

He was wearing a dark suit, with dark matching gloves. His face was painted white, with blue around his eyes, and his hair dyed blue too. The light from outside the door was just enough for Shilo to be able to see enough of him and for his image to be burned into her mind.

She wanted to scream, but she was paralyzed with fear.

Suddenly the clown's gaze crossed the kitchen and stopped at her. Shilo wasn't sure if he could see her or not, but the moment that she felt his eyes connect with hers she let go of the glass of water that was in her hand and watched helplessly as it fell to the tiled floor and shattered near her feet.

When she looked back up to the clown in the window, he was no longer leaning into the glass and looking through it with his hands over his head. Instead, he was now standing up and staring, and Shilo knew at that moment that he saw her too.

The clown then raised a single finger, placed it on the glass, and pointed directly at Shilo before bringing it to his mouth and placing the finger over the center of his lips to make a shooshing motion.

Shilo's heart was racing as the clown suddenly disappeared, stepping sideways out of view. She didn't know where he had gone, or where he was going.

Suddenly there was a knock at the door.

Was it the clown?

Shilo reached for a kitchen knife and ducked below

the counter, peeking just enough over the lip of it to keep the front door in view.

Another knock.

"We know you're in there," a male voice said. "Just come with us peacefully, or we will take you with force. We don't want to have to hurt you."

Shilo stayed kneeling below the counter, holding one hand on her mouth and the knife in the other. She was trembling, her legs and hands both shaking. She didn't know what to do.

That was when Shilo's eyes locked onto the phone on the wall. She ran over to it, picked it up, and then instinctively dialed for help.

No dial tone.

Shilo frantically mashed the buttons several more times with no luck. The phone was disabled, and nobody was going to be coming for help.

"Shit," she whispered to herself, putting the phone back while keeping an eye on the front door.

There was no sign of the clown. He had knocked, but now it was silent.

Shilo thought about what she could do next. The only options were to fight and defend herself or try and hide and wait until the clown left.

The clown said we.

Were there more?

If so, how many?

What was a good hiding spot?

Shilo looked around frantically. The only places that

she could think of were the pantry or hiding upstairs, but either way, she would be cornered and have nowhere to go.

Just then Shilo thought she heard something behind her.

When she turned around and looked across the living room towards the windows that faced the backyard, she could see three other clowns peering into the house.

"Fuck!" she whispered to herself as she clutched the knife tightly in her hand.

The house was surrounded.

Shilo got low to the floor and crawled over to the stairs, trying her best to stay both quiet and out of sight. Just as she bumped into the bottom step, she could hear one of the clowns tapping on one of the glass sliding doors and playing with the handle trying to open it, quickly realizing that it was locked and letting out a grunt of frustration. Just then a shadow appeared at the window by the front door, and the clown that had been knocking and looking in before was now looking through the window once again.

Shilo's heart was pounding in her chest. She thought, briefly, that maybe she was dreaming, but Shilo knew deep down inside that she was not, and she had never felt such terror in all her life. She took a deep breath, trying to remain focused, and then began to ascend the stairs as quietly as she could.

Suddenly there was the sound of a window breaking and then a door sliding open. Shilo froze about halfway up the stairs as she was turning to head up the remaining portion. She glanced over the railing and stared down to the first floor, listening to try and hear anything that she could.

The moonlight that was hitting the back of the house was casting shadows of the clowns who had been standing there across the floor. Shilo could see them stretched across the living room and kitchen area and watched helplessly as they moved slowly around. A few seconds later she could hear glass breaking again, only this time instead of it being a window, it was the sound of someone stepping on broken glass.

That was when Shilo remembered she had dropped her glass of water on the floor in the kitchen.

"Look," a voice said in the kitchen. "Blood."

Blood?

Shilo did not know what the voice was talking about until she looked down and noticed that she had stepped on a piece of glass. She was so distracted from being terrified and with her adrenaline going that she didn't feel the shard of glass in the bottom of her foot. She panicked again, not just because of the injury, but because when she looked down at her injury, she realized there was a trail of blood going up the carpet on the stairs. She felt her heart sink, realizing that the intruders were going to know where she was going easily. She quickly reached down and grabbed onto the glass with her free hand, biting on her tongue hard while she yanked the glass out. She whimpered slightly, using the knife to quickly cut a part of her shirt off to tie tightly around her foot to stop the bleeding.

She knew that she had to get upstairs and hide. It was the only chance she had now, so she took one last glance downstairs, noticing a shadow growing closer to the corner of the kitchen, and then as quietly as she could, made her way up the remaining steps to the second floor. Once there, she could hear someone at the bottom of the steps while at the same time, the front door opened. She frantically looked down both sides of the hallway. Her room was too small and hiding in the hallway closet was not going to be a good option either, so she limped to her parents' bedroom at the far end of the hall. She left the door open but closed it so it was only just slightly ajar thinking that it would be too obvious that was where she was hiding if she closed it all the way and locked it.

Shilo then looked around her parent's room for anywhere that could be a good hiding spot. Her parent's bed was elevated off the floor. She could easily slide underneath, but that was usually always the first place that people looked in the movies. Besides the bed, there was a master bathroom, a large walk-in closet, or a big armoire.

Just then footsteps could be heard at the end of the hall as voices, laughs, and the sounds of furniture and glass being broken came from downstairs.

Taking another deep breath to try and remained focused, Shilo hobbled over to the bathroom. She quickly went in and went right for the medicine cabinet, searching hurriedly for bandages or anything else she could use to wrap her foot up better than it was.

She was lucky that the piece of the shirt held long enough not to leave a trail of blood down the hallway, but it was now drenched, and the blood was dripping onto the bathroom's tiled floor.

There was nothing in the medicine cabinet. Shilo continued to search, moving onto the different drawers and cabinets of the vanity, finally finding gauze and tape in a clear bin along with ointment and other medical supplies. She opened it, quickly taking out the gauze and tape and wrapping her foot up, trying not to make a mess as she could hear the commotion downstairs growing and what sounded like someone ripping her bedroom apart down the other end of the hall.

Once her foot was entirely wrapped up and she tidied up, putting everything back into the drawer and closing it, also making sure to wipe the blood up off the floor, Shilo headed back out into the bedroom. She carefully snuck over to the door, peeking out through the crack she left, and could see someone standing at the end of the hall in the doorway to her room. Suddenly the clown turned around and scratched the back of his head before slowly beginning to make his way down the hall in her direction.

Shilo headed over to the large walk-in closet. When she peered inside, she realized that this was where she was going to have to make her stand. There were plenty of places to hide inside. All her father's large coats on the left and her mother's dresses on the right. The shelves above had more shoes than she had time to count, and all the drawers were probably where her mother kept all her jewelry.

That was when Shilo noticed a pair of her mother's tennis shoes sitting in the corner on the floor. She quickly went over and put them on, lucky that she had the same size shoe. Now she wasn't going to have to worry about her feet being unprotected, and if she could somehow get outside and run, the shoes were going to come in handy.

Just then there was a creaking noise that came from the bedroom, and Shilo knew that the clown that was in the hallway was now opening the door to her parent's room.

 # Chapter 16

Shilo gently pushed her mother's dresses aside as she slipped in between them and hid against the wall, listening carefully to the footsteps in the bedroom. She did not get a chance to close the door to the closet, but she was hoping that it was not going to be too suspicious and that if she were lucky, whoever was walking around would just take a quick look inside and move on.

Wishful thinking.

The footsteps made their way over towards the bathroom first. Shilo could hear the person's shoes on the tiled floor. Whoever it was, was rummaging through the medicine cabinet before quickly sliding the shower curtain over. A second later the shoes were walking across the tiles again and then back into the bedroom. Shilo listened carefully, trying to envision what the person was doing as she could hear them going through some of the drawers of the dressers before opening the big armoire. In what must have been frustration, the doors to the armoire were slammed shut, and a grunt could be heard before whoever was in the bedroom suddenly jumped up onto the bed. They bounced several times, giggling playfully before jumping to the floor. Shilo could then see the person's shadow on the wall as it got lower to the ground, probably checking under the bed before it rose again.

Then the person appeared in the doorway to the closet. They stood at the entrance for a moment, looking around for a few seconds before they took a step inside. Shilo was holding onto the knife as hard as she could, ready to thrust it at a moment's notice. She clutched her mouth with the other, trying to be as quiet as she could as the clown started moving clothes around and ripping things off their hangers.

He started with her father's coats first. After moving them aside several times and throwing a few of them to the floor, he then turned and began to shuffle through her mother's dresses. Shilo knew that even though he was moving quickly, he was being thorough and checking every corner as he continued to move further into the closet, and closer to her.

Just as the clown was about to grab the next handful of dresses to push aside, Shilo couldn't help but take a deep breath, her eyes growing large realizing that in doing so, the clown stopped pushing the dresses and was now looking directly in her direction.

The clown turned his body, ambling until he was now right in front of Shilo. She braced herself as the clown reached forward and began to grab onto the dresses, and just as he yanked them to the side to reveal her hiding behind them, she let out a scream and thrust the knife into him while leaping forward on top of him.

The clown let out a pain-filled grunt as he fell onto the floor with Shilo on top of him. She then got up and began to wildly pull at the shoes above them causing dozens of boxes to drop onto the clown. She used the moment of surprise to run back out into the room, shutting the closet door behind her as the clown inside crashed into it and began to bang on it from the inside.

Shouting could then be heard coming from downstairs, quickly followed by footsteps ascending the stairs.

"Fuck!" Shilo shouted as she held onto the doorknob as best she could, frantically looking around the room for what she might be able to use for a weapon next.

There was a vase on the nightstand.

Shilo knew that she wasn't going to be able to hold the door indefinitely, especially since another intruder was now quickly running down the hallway.

She let go of the doorknob and dove across the bed, running over towards the bathroom and quickly closing the door behind her as the bedroom door flung open. She then locked herself in, looking around for anything that she could use.

Suddenly there was banging on the door. Then the sound of someone kicking it. Shilo quickly grabbed the top of the toilet and then jumped into the tub, closing the shower curtain and raising the piece of porcelain onto her shoulder, ready to strike the second someone touched the curtain.

A second later and the door was smashed open. Then someone entered, and another second later ripped the curtain sideways. Shilo let out a scream and swung the top of the toilet as hard as she could, smacking someone in the side of the head with it. She then quickly sprinted out of the bathroom and into the bedroom. Turning to head towards the bedroom door, she noticed the clown she had stabbed stumbling out of the closet. Just then she was grabbed from behind, and another figure entered the bedroom.

The clown who had been looking through the window by the front door downstairs was now standing in front of her while she struggled to break free of the one holding her from behind that she had struck in the head.

"What do you want from me! Leave me alone!" she screamed, kicking her legs wildly but with no success.

The clown with the blue hair put both his hands up in the air and shrugged his shoulders silently before a smile crossed his face, and he laughed.

"She stabbed me, boss," the clown over by the closet said as he stumbled once more, this time catching himself and sitting on the edge of the bed.

The clown with the blue hair looked over to him, back to Shilo, and then back to the clown again.

Shilo used the distraction to swing her fist at the side of her hip as hard as she could, hitting the clown who was holding her in the groin while grabbing his hand and biting it, causing him to let go of her. The clown with the blue hair turned to try and grab her, but Shilo threw a punch and struck him in the mouth, catching him off guard and causing him to fall forward towards her while she ducked out of the way and then ran out of the room and out into the hallway. She screamed, looking back only once to see that the clowns were giving chase as she tried to get to the staircase as fast as she could.

Her goal was to get downstairs and then make it to the front door. She was hoping that it was still open and that she could just keep running. If she could make it to a neighbor, or hide outside, or flag down someone driving, maybe she could stand a chance at getting away.

As she was rounding the top of the stairs, she ran right into another clown. Not expecting her to run into him, they both flew down the stairs, with Shilo landing on top of him halfway down.

It was painful.

The clown moaned as Shilo got up and quickly ran down the remaining steps.

The front door was slightly ajar.

Shilo, filling with excitement because she was almost there, ran to the front door and flung it open, freezing when she saw what was on the other side.

A giant of a man.

The giant, who smelled of expired meat, was now

towering over her, his smile revealing a mouth full of rotten yellow teeth.

Shilo screamed, turning around instinctively to make a run for the back door. She thought that if she could make it to the backyard now, she might be able to climb the fence into the neighbor's yard in time before any of the clowns could catch her.

She turned and sprinted towards the living room, jumping over the couch as some of the clowns from upstairs, now downstairs, ran through the kitchen after her. She raced for the open and slightly broken glass sliding door only to come to a stop as a clown with his pink hair in spikes, and messy lipstick stepped out of the shadows and was now standing in front of her and blocking her escape.

Quickly turning to try and run past him, he reached out and grabbed Shilo, pulling her arms behind her and forcing her into the middle of the living room where he then threw her onto the couch.

Shilo didn't know what to do. She sat up on the couch, but there was no way out. She looked around while the clowns and the giant were coming from every direction until they were all standing around her.

Then one of them cleared their throats.

When she turned to look behind her, the clown with the suit and blue hair was standing just in between and slightly behind, two of the other clowns. He smiled at her, wiping a little blood from his face where she had punched him, raised his fists mockingly like he was a boxer, and then burst out into laughter.

All of them joined in and laughed with him while Shilo looked at each of their faces unsure of what was coming next.

"What the fuck do you want from me!" Shilo screamed at them, causing them to stop their laughing and all their expressions to turn more serious.

Suddenly the clown in the suit adjusted his tie before he pulled a knife out, raised it, and then held it beside his face with the tip of the blade pointed up. He slowly approached Shilo who didn't know what he was doing. She looked into his dark black eyes as he continued to approach, licking his lips before he suddenly came to a stop and stabbed the couch with the knife over and over until he was out of breath. Hunched over, he slowly rose, tilted his head up to look at her, and then leaned in.

"Boo," he said before they all started laughing again.

Suddenly the attackers all began to come at her and push at her. She tried to deflect their hands as they grabbed at her, managing to land a few punches and scratches on them while a few of them threw punches. Eventually, Shilo was overwhelmed and overpowered, being held down against her will as the clown in the suit had his back to her but was glancing over his shoulder towards the front door.

"Enough fun boys. Let's get moving," he ordered.

Suddenly Shilo noticed a big fist flying through the air at the corner of her eye. It hit her in the side of the head, and everything immediately went black.

***

Shilo awoke in an empty rusty van. She was alone in the back, her hands and feet both bound together by a thick rope. She looked around frantically trying to see if there was anything she could use to cut herself free, but there was nothing of use anywhere in sight. All she could tell besides being in a rusty van was that it was daylight out and that through the filthy windshield, it looked like there was a tree line and perhaps a large tent just outside.

She tried to remember how she got to where she was. Everything was foggy, and she did not know how long she was going in and out of consciousness, but Shilo did vaguely remember a few moments.

First, she remembered being over someone's shoulder and seeing her house for only a brief second before being thrown into the van she could only assume she was still within. Second, she recalled looking around the dark interior of the vehicle while it was moving, surrounded by the clowns and a giant, with the one in a suit in the front passenger seat talking to the driver and occasionally glancing back to her. Third, she could remember the sounds of one of the clowns screaming, in particular, the one that she had stabbed in the shoulder. She saw the others surrounding him and remembered hearing what sounded like them pulling the knife out, and then the distinct sound of the blade hitting the bottom of the van after they removed it from his shoulder.

As hard as Shilo was trying to piece everything together to find out where she was, she had no sense of time or distance. For all she knew, she was out for hours, and they could be anywhere now if the van didn't stop and had continued driving through the night.

Suddenly muffled voices and shouting could be heard outside, soon followed by footsteps and shadows passing by the driver's side window. The commotion grew louder until Shilo could make out that the voices and footsteps were approaching the back of the van. She sat up, scooting herself backward until she was leaning against the back of the front seats.

A lock was opened, and a second later the two doors to the back of the van were pulled open, and Shilo covered her eyes from the sudden burst of sunlight that flooded the van. As she lowered her hands and quickly blinked, her vision slowly adjusting, she saw shadows standing behind the vehicle. When they came into focus, she recognized all of the clowns and the giant that had attacked her in her home including, the one she had stabbed who now had a bandage around his arm, the one she hit in the head with the top of the toilet who now sported a large band-aid on the top of his skull, and the one in the suit with the blue hair who was standing beside someone else she didn't recognize.

He wasn't exactly dressed like the others. He appeared sharper and more refined and was carrying himself differently, with a certain kind of confidence. Besides having some white face paint on, slightly turquoise tinted hair, red eye shadow, and dark lipstick, he was quite handsome and not as scary looking as the other clowns, but rather, he was kind of inviting.

He looked at Shilo for just a few seconds, but it felt like a full minute before he motioned with his head to one of the clowns and they reached in and grabbed Shilo, pulling her to the edge of the van so her legs hung down and she was sitting on the edge. The sharply dressed man then stepped in front of Shilo and looked down at her, tilting her head up gently with one finger under her chin so he could look her in the eyes.

"Hello, sister," he said, as a big smile crossed his face.

Chapter 17

It's been quite a long time, hasn't it?" he said, pulling his finger out from beneath Shilo's chin and taking a step back.

Shilo stared at him in confusion for a few seconds, speechless and in shock.

Was it him?

"I know, I know. It's a lot to process. We can chat later. Right now, I have some other things to attend to," the man said before motioning with his head again to the clown beside Shilo.

The clown then grabbed onto Shilo and lifted her, placing her over his shoulder, and then began to walk off towards the big tent she had noticed through the windshield. As she got further from the van, seeing the man who claimed to be her brother congregating with a few of the other clowns and the giant, she was able to catch a glimpse of where she was before she was taken into the tent.

It was a circus.

Shilo had noticed a large yellow and red striped circus tent off in the distance. It stood out and towered easily over the dozens of other tents scattered around. There didn't seem to be a lot going on however and looked like they were still in the middle of setting everything up.

The clown carrying Shilo threw her to the ground once inside. She landed hard on a rug placed over the ground, and she fell back against what looked like sacks filled with costume props.

"Boss will be with you soon. Stay."

Shilo looked up to the clown who carried her into the tent. He stared down at her, showing his teeth at her in an attempt to intimidate her before he cracked his knuckles, turned around, and then exited the tent, looking like he stopped just outside and was keeping guard.

Shilo looked around. She studied the inside of the tent to try and find anything she could use to cut the rope that she was stuck in. It was so tight that every time she moved, she could feel it digging deeper into her skin, and that made trying to get out of it that much harder.

Sadly, continuing to look around ended up proving to be fruitless. There was nothing but props and chests in the tent. Shilo tried to scoot herself over to one of the chests that were closest to her, but she had no way of lifting the top to see what was inside, and she did not want to make too much noise because she didn't want to bring any more attention to herself than she already had.

The last thing that she wanted was for the clown to come in and hit her, or worse, piss off those who took her and have them kill her before she got a chance to try and escape.

Then Shilo couldn't help but think back to the man who said he was her brother.

Who was he?

Why did he say he was my brother?

Could it really be him?

If so, why was he here and how did he end up like that?

She had so many questions. Each one raised another. She needed answers and needed to know the truth. On top of all of that, and regardless of whatever the truth was, escape was the highest priority.

Just then she heard voices outside. A minute later and someone began to enter the tent.

It was the one who claimed to be her brother.

He took a step in and looked down at Shilo, letting out a sigh before he pulled out a chair from the corner of the room, sat down on it, and then looked over to her.

"It's been quite a while Shilo," he said, a small smirk on his face and now that Shilo was close enough to really look at him, she noticed a familiar look in his eyes.

"Christo-"

"Shh," he whispered, raising a finger to his lips. "I don't go by that name anymore. My name is Jug now."

"Jug?" Shilo inquired, looking down to the ground before looking back up into her brother's eyes. "You disappeared years ago without a trace. What the fuck happened to you?" she inquired, filling with emotion now because she thought for years that the worst had happened to him.

"I ran away is all."

"But why? Do you have any idea of what your disappearing did to mom and dad? What it did to me?"

Jug sat in the chair and leaned back, becoming frustrated as he slammed his fist down onto the chest beside the chair. He then took a deep breath and cracked his neck before leaning back in.

"Mom and Dad never gave a fucking shit about me. You were the golden child Shilo. The smartest, the funniest, and the prettiest. You could never do wrong, and you never did. They always paid attention to you, and they always gave you everything that you needed to succeed."

Shilo's eyes filled with tears while her heart filled with anger.

"That's not true, and you fucking know it! Mom and Dad adored you! You were their only son for god sake. Christo-Jug, whatever the fuck your name is now. The only reason why they were always so hard on you was that they saw the potential in you, but equal in potential, you had uncontrollable anger at the world for no reason!"

Jug sat in his chair, his eyes now big and in shock. He stared at Shilo for a moment before he backhanded her across the face and then stood; glaring down at her while tears began to roll down her cheeks, a red mark slowly starting to appear on one of them.

"Go fuck yourself," she said, spitting at him.

He then raised his hand as if to slap Shilo again. She flinched, and he pulled away, laughing as he walked over towards the entrance of the tent.

"You're going to enjoy your stay here," he said. "Welcome to my circus by the way. I hope you enjoy the show."

Jug laughed again as he exited the tent, leaving Shilo alone once more.

Shilo propped herself up against the chest that she was still sitting next to. She leaned back into it, resting against it so she didn't have to use any strength to hold herself up. She was determined to try and find a way out. She had no idea how she was going to do it. She did not have any plans as of yet, and she didn't know the layout of the circus. She wasn't sure if she was anywhere near an entrance or an exit, but Shilo knew that if she could just manage to get her hands and feet free, even if only her feet, she was confident in her ability to be able to run and getaway. She knew that she needed to be smart about it though. If she were to get caught, there was no telling what the punishment would be.

She was still in shock that her brother was even still alive. She was filled with both anger over how he turned out and sadness that he left and had felt so unloved when it was the furthest thing from the truth. Shilo didn't know what happened to him or what he had been up to over the years. She didn't know how he got into a circus, or what made him even want to be a part of one. Whatever the reasons were, he was the boss and had plenty of other people working under him, and judging by how dangerous and violent they were, it only reinforced that he too was at least equally if not more dangerous and violent himself.

***

Hours passed before an older woman came in. There was no lighting in the tent, so it was hard to tell what she looked like, but Shilo could see that she was older judging by how she was walking and her voice. She had brought Shilo some food and held a bowl out in front of her before dipping a spoon into the bowl and holding it up to Shilo's mouth.

Refusing to take it, and desperate to escape, Shilo pulled away from the spoon and scooted herself away from the old lady before trying to kick at the bowl the lady was holding. She connected, causing the bowl to leave the old woman's hands and fall to the ground and splash all over the rug.

The old lady became enraged. She stood up and let out a shriek before throwing the spoon at Shilo and then grabbing for her head. She took a fistful of Shilo's hair and began to pull her towards the center of the tent while Shilo tried to resist. The old lady then slapped Shilo across the face before going over to where the contents of the bowl had spilled. The old lady pressed her hands into the liquid and then approached Shilo, fighting against Shilo's resistance just enough to be able to wipe her hands all over Shilo's face while Shilo let out a scream.

A few seconds later the clown standing outside came in, and the old lady stood up, exhaling and trying to regain her breath. She stared down at Shilo, and there was now enough light coming in from the flap of the tent being held open by the clown that Shilo was able to see the old lady's face. It was aged, and she wore a toothless grin as she turned and began to laugh as she exited the tent, the clown staring at Shilo for a moment before he too left and she was alone in the dark again.

Shilo was beside herself. Her adrenaline was still going from the old lady attacking her and wiping whatever it was that she was trying to feed her onto her face. It smelled a little like soup, but Shilo couldn't be sure, and she certainly wasn't going to trust eating whatever it was, regardless of how hungry she was.

That was when Shilo thought she recognized something. She sniffed the air, rolling over onto her belly and shimmying herself over to where the liquid had spilled to follow where her scent was taking her. After much struggle, she succeeded in getting over to the wet spot on the rug and smelled it; almost gagging as she quickly turned away and rolled on her other side.

Whatever the liquid was, smelled like blood.

"What the fuck is going on here?" she whispered to

herself.

Something wasn't right. Something was off, but not just about her brother, the clowns, and the old lady, but about the entire circus itself.

***

Shilo listened to wicked laughter and blood-curdling screams throughout the rest of the day and throughout the entirety of the night, only reinforcing her belief that something truly awful was going on.

It wasn't until the sun was rising and its light was breaking slightly through the cloth material of the tent that she was able to notice something different within the tent.

She didn't realize when it had happened, but somehow during the struggle with the older woman, the old lady had dropped some sort of a piece of metal on the ground. Shilo only noticed it because of a small beam of light that was reflecting off it, so she quickly rolled across the ground until she could make out what it was.

Upon further inspection, Shilo could tell that the piece of metal on the ground was a piece of broken jewelry. It didn't look like it was big enough to be a part of a necklace, and it didn't look like it was an earring either. After carefully picking it up with her hands and holding it up to her eyes, she concluded that it looked like a broken ring that was missing its diamond or whatever jewel it had initially contained.

She rolled it back and forth in her fingers until she felt a part of it prick her. Suddenly filled with a rush of adrenaline and excitement, she turned the ring around and began to cut at the ropes on her feet to see if she could do any damage to them.

She could.

It wasn't much and was going to be extremely trivial, but if she worked at it, in a few hours, she thought she might be able to break through and free herself. Once the rope was off her feet, she was hopeful that she could get away from the tent and escape or find something else to cut the rope around her wrists.

***

Several hours later of Shilo working on the rope, she was finally able to cut through a piece of it and cause the rest of it to become loose. It took her exactly as long as she thought it was going to take, but she didn't care because she was another step closer to getting out.

Only once did she have to pause and conceal both the ring and damaged ropes.

A giant, one that looked different than the one who had helped the clowns kidnap her, brought in a bottle of water at one point. He took a sip of it himself before Shilo was willing to drink it, and when she did, she drank the entire bottle without a break for air, which after finishing it, and the giant left, she continued working on the rope.

Now she knew that her feet were free. She didn't have the rope entirely off yet, but it was loose enough that she could kick herself free in a hurry if she needed to. The time to make a move, however, wasn't right for her.

Shilo stayed in the tent, scooted herself as far back as she could go. and listened carefully to a commotion outside. It sounded like a party, followed by cheers and laughter. Soon a clown came in and pulled the cloth for the entrance aside, making sure that no light could enter within. He pulled a knife out and put his finger over his lips while he walked over and sat on the chair that Shilo's brother had used and then stared at her, unmoving, as the sounds of happy families enjoying themselves passed the tent throughout the remainder of the day.

She wanted to scream and get help so badly, but she knew that if she made a noise, the clown would certainly be swift in silencing her, and anyone who came to the aid.

It wasn't until everything fell into darkness again that the wicked laughter and screams off in the distance started once more. The clown left her then, exiting the tent quickly and disappearing into the night.

That was when Shilo quickly kicked her feet free and then stood up, stumbling a few times and struggling to stay upright because of how long she had been tied up. Once she was confident that she was ready to leave, she snuck to the front of the tent and carefully peeked outside. She looked both ways before quickly moving over to the next tent, unsure if she was headed in the right direction but trying her best to go in the opposite direction of where the screams and laughter were coming from.

After passing several tents and peering inside at empty chests, props, and various circus-related items, she managed to find a tent that had a few chests that were closed but had no locks on them. She carefully tiptoed in, opening each one and searching inside until she finally discovered something that she could use.

A knife.

She quickly used it, sawing at the ropes on her wrists until she was able to cut them successfully and they fell to the ground. She breathed a big sigh of relief, rubbing her wrists and staring at the deep cuts, torn flesh, and dried blood they had left behind.

Shilo was trying to keep herself composed. Every part of her wanted to find the closest exit and sprint towards it, but she knew she had to be careful. She had to stay undetected and couldn't get caught, or it would all be over.

Carefully leaving the tent with her newly acquired knife in hand, she continued tent to tent and peering down every path in search of a way out. It wasn't until a few minutes later that she thought she heard a woman crying and a man's voice aggressively telling her to keep quiet. Curious, Shilo carefully made her way closer to the tent where the commotion was coming from. When she peered inside, she could see one of the clowns on top of a woman whose clothes were torn to shreds. He was holding a knife to her throat and forcing himself on top of her, but so far seemed to be unsuccessful in his attempts.

Without hesitation, Shilo rushed into the tent. As the clown turned around, she stabbed him in the throat while the woman he was on top of reached up and grabbed his knife-wielding hand so he couldn't retaliate against Shilo. With a look of surprise in his eyes, Shilo continued to push the knife into his throat as blood began to pour from his gurgling mouth. After several seconds of trying to resist her attack and blood pouring out all over Shilo's hands, his legs began to slowly buckle until he was now lying on the ground and both women were on top of him. The other woman pulled the knife from the clown's hand and began to stab him repeatedly in the chest as Shilo watched the clown's eyes roll into the back of his head, and with a pain-filled exhale, his body went limp.

Shilo stepped back from the clown as the woman continued to stab his dead body and looked down at her blood-soaked hands. She then began to shake a little as the adrenaline started to wear off, but a new sense of purpose came over her as she thought of something.

If her brother had the clowns find her once already, if she escapes, they'll eventually track her down once again.

A chill went through Shilo's body when she realized that escaping might not be enough anymore, especially with what she just interrupted and the women she helped.

How many others were trapped here and needed help?

What other dark, vile, and atrocious acts were going on here?

Somehow Shilo knew that for her to escape and truly be free, she was going to have to take the entire circus down and that she was going to have to end it.

All of it.

Part Five

 # Chapter 18

"Thank you for saving me. My name is Olivia."

"It's a pleasure to meet you, Olivia. My name is Shilo."

The two women sat there in the tent with the bloody corpse of the clown who had tried to rape Olivia. Olivia was sitting next to the clown, while Shilo was standing at the entrance to the tent and peering outside, acting as a lookout and to make sure that nobody had heard the commotion or was coming.

"For now, we are safe, but we can't stay here all night. We have to keep moving, and I need to get you out of here." Shilo said, turning away from the front of the tent and coming over to Olivia, kneeling in front of her as Olivia looked over and stared at the dead clown, his lifeless eyes staring up at the ceiling of the tent.

"Where are we going to go?"

"We aren't going anywhere, it's just you," Shilo replied.

Olivia looked over to Shilo who was still crouched in front of her and locked eyes.

"What do you mean?"

"Once I get you out of here, run for help. I'll be coming back and doing whatever I can to destroy this circus."

"Wouldn't that be easier to let the police handle it?"

Shilo nodded, glancing over her shoulder as the sound of voices approached. She held a finger up to her mouth to signal to be quiet, and Olivia and Shilo watched as two clowns walked past the tent. They continued walking without stopping or noticing Shilo and Olivia. Their voices slowly fading away the further they got until the women could no longer hear them.

"It would be easier to let the police handle it, but I can't risk it. There are more people here who need help. Waiting for the cops to get here might be too long. I need to help them while I can, and I can't let *him* escape."

Olivia looked at Shilo puzzled, wondering who she was referencing.

"Who is *him*?"

"Christo-Jug. He is the leader of whatever the fuck this place is and the reason why I'm even here to begin with. I can't let him escape. I need to make sure this ends, tonight."

"Well, I'm not going to let you do this on your own. They already killed one of my friends," Olivia announced. "I don't know where the other one is. So, until I find her, I'm not leaving either."

Shilo looked at Olivia, and after a few seconds, nodded that she agreed.

"Okay, we're in this then. Together."

Olivia nodded back and then Shilo reached out with her hand, Olivia grabbed it, and Shilo pulled her up. They embraced each other for a moment, looking down at the bloodied clown before both looking at the knives they held and then headed towards the front of the tent with Shilo leading the way.

Shilo glanced out, carefully looking both ways down the path outside. Once she was sure it was clear, she crouched and began to move into the shadows in between the tents opposite of them. Once she was on the other side, she waved for Olivia to follow.

An occasional scream echoed in the air every few minutes. Some were from women, some were from men, and some were not audible enough to tell. Shilo and Olivia slowly made their way towards one of the screams, bringing them closer to the tree-line and further from the big top tent off in the distance. Once they thought they were in the right area, they listened, trying to pinpoint where the scream they followed had come from, finally finding a bright red tent with candlelight emanating from it and muffled moans coming from inside. They approached slowly, being careful not to make any noises and making sure that they stuck to the shadows.

As they finally got next to the tent, they listened carefully to what was going on inside. The muffled moans were followed by what sounded like a wet sawing noise. Shilo and Olivia had no idea what was going on. Shilo got down on the ground, peering underneath the material of the tent to look inside before raising her hand with just a single finger pointed up. After she was up off the ground, she and Olivia slowly made their way to the entrance of the tent. Shilo slowly counted to three, giving a hard nod on three, and with that the two women entered the tent with their weapons at the ready.

Just as quickly as they had entered, they came to a stop, frozen in shock with what they were looking at and trying to comprehend what was going on.

There was blood splatter on every wall of the interior of the tent as a rope with what looked like intestines thrown over them traveled from one side of the tent to the other. At the center of the tent was a table with a man on it. He was chained down with a rag in his mouth and rope keeping it and his head in place. Beside him was a fat man with his back turned to the women, making a sawing motion with his one arm while the other seemed to be holding something in place. The man on the table was moaning, and his expression was one filled with agony. Suddenly his eyes opened, and he glanced over, noticing Shilo and Olivia standing in the entrance of the tent with their knives in hand. He began to moan wildly, trying to scream and visibly distraught in an attempt to get the women to intervene and help him. The man who was sitting beside him noticed this, and looked over to him, realizing that he was looking at something and reacting to it.

Shilo and Olivia looked over at each other before turning back to the man who was now slowly turning around in his seat. As he rotated, what became revealed was a large saw in one hand and a now detached lower right forearm in his other, and with that, it became obvious that he was cutting the man to pieces while he was still alive.

The man now fully turned, facing, and staring at Olivia and Shilo, let out an annoyed grunt that he was interrupted. As he slowly rose to his feet, he threw the man's forearm into a nearby bucket that also contained two severed lower legs and someone else's head.

Before he could do anything else, Olivia and Shilo both charged at the man, colliding into him with their knives and hitting him with such combined force that all three of them crashed into the table with the man on it and flipped over him, landing hard on the ground on the other side. The butcher struggled to try and get up while Shilo and Olivia repeatedly stabbed him in the back and neck, trying their hardest not to scream or make any noise. After a minute of countless stabs, the two women fell over exhausted and panting, the butcher's lifeless body face-down on the ground and bleeding profusely from all of the stab wounds he received.

As Shilo and Olivia tried to compose themselves and catch their breath, carefully listening and trying to tell if their commotion caught the attention of anyone who might be nearby, Shilo double-checked the butcher for any signs of life. After examining him by checking for a pulse, she glanced back to Olivia and shook her head before turning and looking up to the man who was still on top of the table.

Shilo slowly rose, walking around the table and examining the man while Olivia followed and joined her side. They looked down at the bound and savagely mutilated man who was staring up at the ceiling of the tent and in a state of agonal breathing.

Olivia covered her mouth in horror as Shilo tried to comfort the man, stroking his head as he closed his eyes and took one long last breath before he exhaled and passed.

"Fuck," Shilo said as she lowered her head.

Olivia turned away and couldn't look, thinking about what must have been going through his mind during his final moments and the immense amount of pain he must have been suffering.

"What the fuck kind of place is this?" Olivia whispered as she looked down at the bucket of limbs before suddenly feeling sick.

"Hell," Shilo said as she stepped next to Olivia and placed a hand on her shoulder. "Are you okay?" she inquired checking Olivia to make sure she wasn't injured at all.

"I'm okay," Olivia replied.

Just then another scream came from outside, this time a woman's.

"That was close," Shilo announced, walking towards

the front of the tent and looking out through the opening.

The scream sounded out again.

"I know that scream," Olivia broke, rushing to the front and trying to exit the tent but Shilo grabbed her and stopped her.

"What are you doing? We have to go help!" Olivia pled while Shilo tried to calm her.

"And we will, but we can't rush in. It could be a trap, or we could risk getting ourselves caught. We must be smart about this. Just try to stay calm and follow my lead. Okay?"

Olivia stared into Shilo's eyes before taking a deep breath and calming herself. She knew that Shilo was right and that they couldn't just rush in, but every second counted and if it was any reflection on what Shilo and she just witnessed, they couldn't waste any more time.

Shilo led the way out of the tent again, continuing into the shadows before heading in the direction of the screams. As they passed a few tents, Shilo was able to notice a tall metal fence just by the trees, and as they continued to move and search for the source of the screaming, she realized that the fence must go around the entire circus.

A minute passed before the screams were close. Shilo held up her hand to signal Olivia to wait. A second later they were on the move again and sprinted across a dirt path, jumping over several ropes holding a bigger tent down and then running alongside it before stopping at its end.

Just behind the bigger tent was a small clearing with a bunch of tables scattered around. It looked like a food area where people could sit and enjoy food from the nearby concession stands, but because the circus was closed, so too were they.

Standing on one side of the table was a clown with a big metal baseball bat in his hand. On the other side of the table was a young girl with long blonde hair and who was covered in dirt. She was gasping for breath, and every time the clown giggled or moved around the table, she screamed and jumped in the opposite direction. He was toying with her and seemed to be enjoying every moment of it.

"That's Emma!" Olivia whispered in shock confirming that she did, in fact, know who the screams had been coming from. "We have to help her."

Shilo nodded as she looked around the clearing.

Olivia knew that Shilo was looking around to check that they were alone first before they revealed themselves. Jumping out too hastily wasn't going to benefit anybody. Second, Olivia knew that they didn't have much time to try to intervene. They were going to have to be quick, but they also had to be sure they attacked when the clown's guard was down. Emma didn't have a weapon by the looks of it, so it was going to be just her and Shilo again.

"We have to be fast," Shilo whispered. "We're going

to be out in the open. We must hurry and make sure we catch him off guard. On the count of three okay?"

Olivia nodded.

"One."

Olivia took a deep breath.

"Two."

An exhale.

"Three."

As soon as Shilo finished her count, the two of them charged out into the open. They ran across the dirt towards the clown who was beginning to circle the table. Just as Shilo lifted her knife, Emma looked over and noticed them quickly approaching.

"Olivia?" she said in shock.

The clown, now alarmed, turned and looked over his shoulder and noticed Olivia who stopped dead in her tracks and became paralyzed with fear.

"Well, well. What do we have here?"

Just as the clown turned to face Olivia, Shilo thrust her knife into his side. He gasped in shock and spun around, swinging his bat in Shilo's direction and connecting with her shoulder. She stumbled and fell over, still holding onto the knife and pulling it out as she fell to the ground.

The clown let out a yell and clutched his side, hunching over onto one knee before raising his bloody hand and looking down at it.

That was when Olivia made her move. She quickly ran at the clown, but before she could do anything, the clown anticipated this and swung the end of his bat to his side, hitting Olivia in the gut and causing her to stumble back and throw up on the ground.

As the clown slowly stood, his legs wobbly for a brief second, he walked towards Olivia and rose his bat above his head preparing to bring it down on her.

Olivia raised her arm to shield herself while still retching from getting hit in the gut.

Suddenly someone jumped on top of her and all Olivia could hear was the sound of the bat striking something with a loud thud as someone let out a muffled pain-filled shout. A second later and Olivia realized that Shilo had jumped on top of her and had taken the bat to her back.

Shilo rolled off Olivia, one arm behind her back and rolling around in pain as the clown looked down at the two of them, laughing, while blood continued to pour from his wound on the side of his chest.

He slowly began to walk towards them, mumbling something to himself while raising his bat above his head again. Olivia knew that this time he wasn't going to miss her and all she could do was hold her arms up to protect herself.

Just as quickly as the clown's arms began to come down, they stopped.

He let out a grunt, and his face twitched as he then fell to one knee.

Standing behind him was Emma, and she had Shilo's knife in her hand.

Olivia knew that it was now or never. She quickly got to her feet and charged at the clown, thrusting the knife into his throat as she pushed into him and the clown fell onto his back. She continued to stab him, with Emma joining in before she felt a hand on her shoulder and looked up to see who it was.

It was Shilo, and she was standing beside her and Emma with the clown's bat clutched in her hands.

"Step aside," she said sternly.

Emma and Olivia both moved out of the way as Shilo quickly swung the bat and brought it down on the clown's face. After the first hit, she let out an aggressive grunt before continuing to swing the bat and striking the clown in the head over and over again. She continued to hit him at least a dozen times more before all that remained of the clown's head was a pile of smashed bone and brain matter, with some of it dripping off the end of the bat.

Shilo then collected herself and let out a deep sigh.

"This is one of the clowns that kidnapped me," she announced as she spat at the body.

Just then several shouts could be heard off in the distance.

"We need to get out of here," Olivia announced.

"We can't leave the body out in the open either," Shilo returned.

"What do we do?" Emma asked, still in shock and holding the knife in her hand.

"Olivia, help me move the body. Emma, try to cover

this mess up with the dirt. Move it around as best as you can and try to cover the blood up, quickly. I'm not ready for them to know we're hunting them down yet. We need to keep the element of surprise."

Everyone agreed and did what was asked of them. While Shilo and Olivia dumped the body of the clown behind one of the concession stands and happened to find a couple of bags of grain to hide him behind, Emma moved the dirt around in an attempt to cover up the mess.

Once everyone regrouped in the clearing, Shilo led the way out of the area and back into the shadows as the shouts that were once off in the distance, were soon in the area of the clearing which Shilo was now leading the women in the opposite direction of.

Chapter 19

After finding a tent to hide in for a few minutes, the women tried to come up with a plan on what to do next.

"Now that I helped you find your friend, it's time I help you find a way out of here," Shilo said to Olivia as she continued to keep an eye out at the front of the tent.

"I'm not leaving you. Not now, I can't. We need each other," Olivia replied.

"She needs you now," said Shilo who pointed over to Emma who hadn't said a word since they left the clearing and who was sitting next to Olivia silently rocking back and forth.

Emma was in shock, and Olivia knew that Emma wasn't going to be of any use to anyone if they got caught and had to fight again. She was in no condition to do anything, and Shilo was right, Emma wasn't going to be able to escape on her own and needed Olivia's help.

"She'll be okay," Olivia said, reaching over and brushing some of Emma's blonde hair out of her eyes.

"How's your back though?" she inquired, looking over to Shilo who was rubbing it with her one free hand.

"It's sore, but I'll live."

A few seconds of silence passed before Shilo left the front of the tent and sat on the other side of Emma.

"We have to try and find a way out of here. I noticed a fence on the other side of the tents. It looked too hard to climb, but if we can find a way under or a gate, maybe we stand a chance if it's not being watched."

Olivia agreed.

"When do you think we should try to find that?" Olivia asked.

"Soon. I think Emma should rest for a few more minutes."

"I-I'm fine," Emma said, finally speaking and snapping out of the trance she was in.

"Are you sure you're ready? We can wait a little bit," Shilo reassured.

After a few seconds, Emma nodded, turning to look at Olivia first and then Shilo with a smile on her face.

"I can do this. I'll be okay. I just want to get out of here."

Shilo looked over to Olivia and nodded before moving to the front of the tent and looking outside. A moment later she motioned with her hand, and Olivia moved to go towards her but suddenly felt a hand grab hers and caused her to stop. When Olivia glanced back, she realized that Emma had reached out and was holding onto her hand. She knew that Emma was scared, and she squeezed her hand to reassure her that she was there, and with that Emma began to follow too.

They exited the tent slowly, moving together as they pushed through a bush, and then Olivia noticed the fence that Shilo had mentioned.

It was tall and metal, with the bars too close together to squeeze through and the top of the fence at a weird angle which made it an impossibility to try and climb.

Shilo was right in that they had to find a gate or somewhere they could slip under.

"This way," Shilo announced as she moved around a bunch of boxes and hugged the fence, squeezing herself in between a bunch of barrels before continuing forward. Olivia was next and followed, with Emma hesitant at first but eventually pulling through as well. Shilo then proceeded to lead the way, passing several more tents before suddenly coming to a stop behind a large crate and putting her finger over her mouth.

She looked over the crate for a few seconds before quickly ducking down. Her eyes grew big, and Olivia was curious to know what she had seen. She began to slowly move towards the crate so she could get a look too, but Shilo stuck her hand out to stop her.

A few seconds later someone walked by completely unaware that the three of them were just a few feet away.

Once the person was out of sight, the three women exhaled in relief as Shilo looked back over the crate and motioned for Olivia and Emma to join her. After peeking over the crate, Olivia could see what Shilo had discovered.

It was a gate.

About twenty yards away there was a group of vehicles. Two trucks, a car, and a rusty old-looking van parked next to each other and just beyond them, a large open gate with two tall men standing guard.

"Finally, a way out," Olivia whispered.

"If I can distract those guards, the two of you should easily be able to get away."

"How are we going to do that?" Emma asked.

"I haven't figured that out yet," Shilo responded as she stepped away from the crate and began to look and see what was in the immediate area. She turned around and looked back to Emma and Olivia with a look of determination in her eyes.

"Got an idea?" Olivia asked.

Shilo nodded.

"Wait here. I'm going to cause a distraction and get the guards to follow. When they do, both of you need to run and don't stop until you get to safety. Get the police too."

Olivia and Emma both nodded as Shilo ran across the small trail and dove into a tent. Olivia then noticed her slip out the back of the tent and then move behind another, this time disappearing entirely out of view. Olivia then turned to Emma and grabbed her hand, squeezing it for reassurance while the two women peered over the box and stared at the guards by the gate.

Olivia and Emma didn't know what Shilo was up to. Neither of them knew what kind of a distraction she was going to be doing, but all they could do now was trust in her and wait.

Just then a scream rang out, but it didn't belong to Shilo. It was a man's scream. Olivia and Emma both turned in the direction it was coming, which wasn't in the direction that Shilo had gone.

"Who was that?" Emma said with a gasp, her eyes large and full of surprise.

"I have no idea," Olivia responded, she too caught off guard and curious.

Suddenly there was the sound of a loud crash. It sounded like something big and heavy fell over and then the sounds of shouting followed.

Olivia leaned over and looked down the path in an attempt to see what the commotion was all about, and after a few seconds, she noticed that someone was running in their direction. She quickly huddled back next to Emma, and the two of them got as low as they could unsure of who was coming.

The sound of panting and heavy breathing approached, soon stopping as incoherent mumbles could be heard. Olivia wanted to move over and see what was happening, but she didn't want to risk exposing her and Emma's hiding place. All she could do was stay put and stare at what little of the path she could see in between some of the other smaller boxes nearby.

As the incoherent mumbling continued, a pair of feet came into view, stepping sporadically around as if lost. It was apparent that whoever it was didn't know where they were, or they were intoxicated in some way. Olivia stretched herself a little, just enough to be able to see through the cracks of two other boxes, and could see a young man in a bloody shirt that was frantically looking around. She wondered if he too had been kidnapped like her, Shilo, Emma, and some of the other individuals whose screams could be heard randomly throughout the night.

Olivia was just in the middle of whispering something and out to the man when shouts sounded out from the direction that he had come from.

"There he is!" a voice announced.

The man who Olivia was sure had heard her froze, and within seconds was trading punches with someone before being tackled to the ground. He was now on his stomach, and someone was on top of him that Olivia could just barely make out was a clown. He struggled to hold the young man down who had now locked eyes with Olivia. Just as he went to go and reach his arm out towards her, the clown on top of him punched him in the head several times before then beginning to slam his head into the dirt. A second later another pair of feet appeared and came to a stop beside the clown. The clown stopped hitting the man, leaning back and releasing his head but continuing to stay on top of him.

The man picked his head up from the dirt and looked over to the large feet. He stared at them for a second, his eyes slowly rising as if to see who the feet belonged to before he suddenly let out a scream. Mid-scream, one of the big feet disappeared upwards out of view only to quickly return as it came down on the screaming man's head with such brute force that the man's head caved in and his body immediately went limp.

Olivia covered her mouth in horror, watching as the foot rose and returned to the path revealing scattered teeth and a pile of crushed flesh with bits of skull fragments and brain matter with a lone popped-out eyeball beside it.

Almost throwing up while wanting to scream at the same time Olivia bit her tongue and looked away, knowing that she and Emma would be killed on the spot if they were discovered.

Suddenly a woman began to shout off in the direction of the gates.

It was Shilo.

"Hey, you fuckers! Over here!" Shilo screamed, jumping up and down out in the open.

The clown and other individuals near Olivia and Emma took off running in Shilo's direction. As they left, Olivia and Emma quickly moved to the crate and looked over it, watching as the two guards at the gate joined the two men. They chased after Shilo who was already out of view and probably running for her life.

"Now is our chance!" Emma said as she sprung up,

but Olivia grabbed her and pulled her back down.

"Wait!" she whispered, dismissing the chance to escape that was currently open.

"We can't just leave her," Olivia said.

"She told us to! If we don't get away her distraction was all for nothing!" Emma said, tugging on Olivia's arm.

"Wait just a few more seconds. Please?" Olivia begged, hoping that by some miracle she could get a sign that Shilo had at least gotten away from those pursuing her.

Suddenly there was a noise in the tent across the path and next to the dead body of the young man Olivia witnessed die. A shadow was moving, and then it suddenly sprang into view.

It was Shilo.

"Move!" she shouted as she quickly ran at the two women in cover.

Olivia and Emma quickly took off running, headed straight for the gate as fast as they could with Shilo close behind. Olivia was sprinting as fast as she could, keeping an eye out and looking around frantically to see if anyone was watching or giving chase.

After getting to the gate and facing a small field with a dirt road and trees on the other side, Shilo stopped at the entrance. Olivia also stopped while Emma continued to run a few more steps before she too was standing in place.

"You can still come with us!" Olivia begged, hoping

that a part of Shilo would come around and that she would leave with her and Emma.

Shilo shook her head no and looked down at the knife in her hand.

"I can't. I need to stop this. I need to stop Jug."

"The police can take care of him Shilo. You don't need to do this!"

"Yes, I do. It's my responsibility. I can't risk letting Jug getaway."

"Why? Why is this man so important to you?" Emma jumped in.

"Because, he's my brother," Shilo revealed, Olivia and Emma glancing at one another in shock before looking back to Shilo who was already sprinting back through the gate and in the direction of the tents.

"C'mon Olivia, let's go! If she has a death wish, let her be. That's on her, not us!" Emma said as she ran up to Olivia and shook her shoulders.

Olivia watched as Shilo disappeared out of view before turning back to Emma and shaking her head.

"I can't let her do this herself. I owe her that much. You need to keep going. You can escape, and you can survive. Find help and get the police. That's what you need to do."

Emma stared into Olivia's eyes before giving her a quick hug.

"Go!" Olivia shouted as Emma flinched before reluctantly turning around and then running through the field towards the trees. "We're counting on you,

Emma. Run!"

As Emma disappeared into the trees, Olivia turned and ran back through the gates. She paused, letting out a sigh as she glanced back across the field in the direction that Emma had gone before turning back towards the tents nearby and the big top off in the distance.

"Okay Shilo, where did you go?" she whispered to herself.

Suddenly shouting began to approach, so Olivia quickly took off running in the direction that she thought Shilo had gone in an attempt to try and find her.

 # Chapter 20

Olivia stayed in the shadows as much as she could; being cautious when crossing the paths and making sure she was quick to get back into cover. She was desperately trying to find Shilo. She knew that they were stronger and stood a better chance at survival if they stuck together. Going at it alone was not an option, not anymore.

While Emma was off running through the woods and would hopefully find help and get it to come, Olivia knew that it might be a while before help arrived. It wasn't going to be instant, and so she was going to need to find Shilo, find this Jug character, do what they needed to do, and then try to hold on for as long as they could.

"Olivia!"

Just as Olivia was passing by a tent, she heard a whisper calling out from the darkness within. When she turned and slowly approached it, Shilo leaned out and revealed her face. She motioned to Olivia, and after making sure it was clear, she quickly darted inside.

Shilo closed the cloth at the front of the tent before turning to Olivia with a look of confusion on her face.

"What are you doing here? Where's Emma?" she inquired with concern.

"Emma went for help. I wasn't going to leave you alone. I had to come back to help you. I owe you that much for saving me."

"You don't owe me anything," Shilo whispered back, quickly glancing outside out of instinct. "But since you're here, there's nothing I can really do about it now, huh?"

Olivia shook her head.

"So, do you have a plan? You said you're looking for your brother. What the hell is that all about?"

"It's a long story, so I'll try to make it short. He ran from home years ago. We thought the worst and moved on with our lives. It turns out he had joined the circus and has had a secret vendetta against me. He had me kidnapped, and now I'm here. I know he'll find me again somehow so I can't just leave. I can't let anyone else get hurt by him or his choices."

Olivia nodded as she tried to comprehend everything that Shilo was revealing to her. It was insane that any of them were even in the situation that they were, but to have the leader and person behind everything that was going on be her brother? That was something else entirely.

"As for a plan, I'm not really sure I have one. My main goal was to help you and Emma escape. Now that we're past that, I'm just trying to make my way closer to that big monstrosity of a tent over there," Shilo said, pointing in the direction of the big top. "If he's anywhere, it has to be somewhere near there. What I'm going to do and how I'm going to go about doing it I don't exactly know yet."

Suddenly a scream rang out. Both women tightened their grips on their knives, and after checking outside, Shilo sprinted out of the tent with Olivia close behind.

They ran down the path, quickly diving behind several barrels being used for garbage cans as two clowns appeared in front of a tent further up ahead. After watching the clowns reach into the tent they were near and pull out a woman, Shilo quickly got up and entered into a long yet open makeshift structure that looked like a dining area with tables and chairs scattered around. She slowly stalked the clowns, Olivia practically glued to her hip. They stayed as low as possible and just below the tops of the tables but still able to see what the clowns were up to.

They held the woman by her arms, occasionally punching her while laughing hysterically at her attempts to try and break free. She screamed and screamed, flailing her legs wildly in the area as one of the clowns leaned over and licked the side of her face. She proceeded to then spit at the clown who retaliated with a punch to her stomach, causing her to collapse forward and begin to dry heave.

Olivia looked to Shilo for direction. She didn't know

what Shilo might be planning. She wasn't sure if she was going to charge out and ambush the clowns like they had done a few times already, or if perhaps how bad the last clown fight went, maybe Shilo would somehow approach this one differently. Either or, they needed to hurry because the clowns were beginning to become more aggressive with the woman and Olivia wasn't sure how much longer she was going to last.

The woman was now on her back and in the dirt. One of the clowns was kicking her while the other looked on and continued to laugh hysterically, he too occasionally joining in and kicking her as well.

"You circle that way," Shilo commanded, pointing off to the right where the tents were. "I'll keep going this way. Wait for me to make the first move."

Olivia had an idea of what Shilo was doing. She was probably going to attack from one side while she knew that Shilo wanted her to attack from the direction of the tents.

Moving swiftly and without a sound, Olivia made her way behind the tents, moving slowly and carefully watching the spot where the clowns were while looking around and making sure no one else was coming. She could see Shilo still crouched behind the tables, but she was slowly making her way to the clown who had his back to her and was still laughing at the woman's pleas for mercy.

Just then, Shilo reached up and around from behind the clown and jammed her knife into the side of his neck. She could hear his muffled scream as Shilo brought the blade across his neck until it exited the other side, blood now pouring from his wide-open throat as he fell to the ground and clutched his hands around his neck.

Shilo stood there over his body as the other clown, now realizing that the other one had abruptly stopped his laughing, slowly turned his attention away from the woman he was beating.

That was when Olivia sprung her attack.

The clown took only three steps in Shilo's direction before Olivia's knife was piercing the side of the clown's head just behind the ear. She had been aiming for his neck and missed, but still hit her target, plunging the knife as far into the clown's skull as she could while he spun and grabbed her, both of them falling to the ground. As they both collided with the ground, Olivia was quick to roll over and begin to stand back up while the clown was now lying motionless and blood began to form a pool underneath him. When he fell, his head hit the ground on the side where the knife was, driving it further into his skull and to the point where all that remained visible of the knife was its wooden handle.

Shilo and Olivia both turned their attention to the woman, both running over to her and trying to comfort her as she continued to flail her limbs around as if still trying to fend off an attacker like the clowns were still there.

"Hey, hey, you're okay," Olivia comforted while Shilo

was trying to combat the woman's hands in an attempt to get her to stop swinging.

"Everything is going to be okay now. You're safe," Shilo said in a composed tone, causing the woman to begin to slow down her defensive guard finally.

After a few more seconds of attempting to calm the woman, she settled down and then leaned into Olivia and began to sob uncontrollably. Olivia wrapped her arms around the woman to console her while Shilo stood up and looked around.

"We need to get out of here, quick," Shilo said as she reached down and attempted to try and pull the woman to her feet.

Olivia got up and tried to help as the confused woman began to look around frantically unsure of what was going on.

"Wh-what's going on?" she said in between the tears.

"Someone's coming. We must get out of here. *Now*."

Shilo quickly took off in the direction of the big top tent pulling on one of the girl's arms while Olivia aided and pursued after. They got away from the dead clowns as fast as they could, suddenly dipping down another path and following a row of large dark-colored tents until they came to the paths end at a large cage on wheels that looked like it was for a large animal, but currently, there was nothing inside of it. They hid behind it in the grass while trying to catch their breath as the sudden sound of yelling coming from where they had just run from broke out.

Shilo and Olivia looked on as the shouting only grew louder, and they could see a few clowns pass by and come out of a few tents further down the path. They were all headed off in the direction of where they had just fought.

"I counted at least three more," Shilo said. "That's not including the two guards who were at the gate and the other two or three I had chasing me from earlier."

"So at least five?" Olivia thought out loud. "And Jug."

"And Jug," Shilo repeated, glancing over to Olivia with a nod. "I know there is an old woman around here somewhere too. I just don't know where she is."

"I've seen her too. I don't know where she is either," Olivia seconded.

"I do," the other woman said, suddenly appearing to be out of her state of hysteria and pointing in a direction just off to their right. "She's in the big brown tent not far from here actually. It's really old-looking."

Olivia and Shilo stared at her for a few seconds surprised.

"Thank you," Shilo said. "What's your name by the way?"

"Hayley," she replied.

Shilo nodded as she and Olivia introduced themselves before a group of clowns passed by further down the path.

"Their searching for us," Olivia announced.

"But they don't know how many of us there are," Shilo added. "We have the advantage."

"What do you mean?" Hayley inquired.

Shilo sighed.

"We aren't trying to escape," she said. "We're trying to rescue anyone we come across and destroy this circus and everyone involved with it."

Hayley's eyes grew large as her hands began to shake. When she noticed that Olivia and Shilo saw her hands, she quickly placed them underneath herself and sat on them to try and hide them.

"It's okay," Shilo comforted. "You're in shock over the situation. We've all had our moment. We're all going to get through this, we just need to find a place for you to stay low and hide unless you want to come with us and fight."

"I-I-I don't think I can fight," Hayley stuttered, her face beginning to lose color as she began to look around frantically.

Olivia leaned over to place her hand on Hayley's shoulder to try and calm her down, but Hayley suddenly smacked Olivia's hand away and stood up, catching her and Shilo off guard. She stepped out onto the path and suddenly began to scream wildly.

"Here! We are over here!" she began to shout, waving her arms in the air.

"What the fuck!" Olivia shouted as Shilo quickly grabbed her hand and began to pull Olivia off in the opposite direction.

Hayley stayed where she was and continued to scream and make a scene as shouting quickly approached. Shilo was running as fast as she could while making sure to keep a tight grip on Olivia's hand. Olivia was trying her best to keep up, but Shilo was much faster, however, Olivia knew that Shilo wasn't going to leave her behind no matter what.

"They went that way!" Hayley could be heard screaming over and over until she let out a blood-curdling scream.

Then there was only silence.

 # Chapter 21

Shilo and Olivia did not understand why Hayley had done what she did. They could not think why she stood up and started to scream and give away their position when they had just fought and saved her from her captor's moments earlier.

Maybe she couldn't handle it Olivia thought, or perhaps something inside Hayley snapped and couldn't face either being left alone or having to fight and do what it was going to take to survive. All Olivia could do now was hope that she and Shilo could get away and find a place to hide and hopefully not be found. If they were to get cornered or captured, it was going to be a fight to the death for both of them.

Suddenly Shilo turned down a smaller path and then came to a stop. In front of them was a large old looking brown tent. After hesitating for just a few seconds, Shilo led Olivia over towards it, approaching the front cautiously before peering inside.

Towards the back of the tent was the sound of chanting. It was almost hard to hear, but whoever it was would occasionally hit something that gave off a strange metallic noise.

Olivia and Shilo stared at each other before they both took a step into the tent. With each of them carrying a knife, they both committed to facing whatever and whoever they would find inside together.

The inside of the tent was dark. If it were not for the dozens of lit candles in the corners of the tent, it would be pitch-black inside. There was a table with chairs beside it just a few feet in, and behind that what appeared to be a wall of beads. Beyond that was where the chanting was coming from.

Shilo and Olivia circled the table, approaching the wall of beads slowly and trying their hardest not to make any noise. Once they were reunited at each other's side and against the wall of beads, they looked through them and could see the shadow of someone sitting on the ground with their back to them. They were wearing a cloak like the old lady had been seen in and were surrounded by dimly lit candles and chanting in a low tone, reaching over with their right arm and tapping on something metallic that looked like a little bell, but didn't sound like any bell that Olivia had ever heard before.

Holding her hand up and slowly raising her fingers, one at a time, Olivia watched Shilo's signal, lunging forward with her towards the shadow in the room as soon as Shilo's third finger rose up. They both landed on the figure, stabbing at it with both of their knives over and over as several candles got knocked over in the process and the tent began to catch on fire. The shadow they landed on began to scream, revealing that it wasn't the old lady, but rather a clown in disguise that Olivia caught a glimpse of his face while they were stabbing him. As he laid there bleeding, and his cloak caught on fire, Shilo and Olivia quickly fled out of the back of the tent.

Olivia and Shilo stared on, the warmth from the heat hitting them in the face as the screams of the clown inside could be heard coming from within the tent that was now completely engulfed in flames and that had collapsed in on itself. As shouting began to approach the area, the two women took off running, this time weaving in and out of the tents and another area of concession stands as they headed in the direction of the big top.

The women came to a stop in an area that had a variety of game stands. They picked a random one and ran to the side, trying the door and entering within once it opened. They then crawled on the ground so they were out of sight and huddled together beside a pile of large teddy bears that were surely used for prizes.

"What the fuck was that all about?" Olivia whispered still wondering what had happened back at the tent and why there was a clown disguised as the old lady.

"I have no idea," Shilo returned in between large breaths as she tried to make sense of what happened as well. "It's like she knew we were coming, and she set a trap for us.

"Do you think that Jug knows yet? Do you think we will still be able to find him?"

Shilo nodded.

"I have a feeling that he didn't go anywhere. This is his circus. I doubt he's gone anywhere. Where he is, I have no idea, but I'm certain that we will find him. I will not stop looking for him, even if I have to burn down every single fucking tent in this entire place and search through the ashes. I will find him, and this will end tonight. There is nowhere he can hide. I'm coming for him."

"We're coming for him," Olivia added.

Shilo smirked slightly, rubbing one of her arms and revealing a small burn she must have received in the most recent fight.

That was when Olivia noticed that she had one as well, only on the side of her leg.

"This place is going to be the death of us," Olivia said.

"Probably," she chuckled. "Just as long as it's all of their graves as well," she said, pointing over towards the top of the counter they were hiding beneath.

The two women covered their mouths and giggled as they could smell smoke in the air. Moments later shouting began to come from all over as several people ran by.

Now curious about what was going on, the two women cautiously rose up and peered over the edge of the counter of the game stand, the sight of a rapidly spreading wall of fire meeting their gaze.

The fire that they had started at the old woman's tent had spread to other nearby tents and was now making its way across the entire circus, jumping from structure to structure.

"Holy fuck," Shilo whispered.

Olivia could only watch in awe, not sure how to react. It was the first time she had ever seen a fire like that. While amazed by the beauty of it, a part of her was also concerned because a part of her knew that if the fire continued to spread like it was, there soon wouldn't be anywhere to hide at all.

"We need to get out of here," Shilo announced, pointing to the door.

Just as she and Olivia were about to move, Shilo froze as a voice neared outside that was barking orders. Shilo looked over the counter and then quickly ducked down, her eyes large as she gripped tightly onto the knife she was holding with both hands.

Olivia was unsure of what she saw until she quickly looked over the top of the counter and saw a group of clowns and two giant men standing next to a well-dressed man with a top hat who was yelling at them. He began to point at the fire, yelling and screaming orders at some of the clowns until they ran off towards it with buckets of water which were certainly not going to be enough to quell the flames.

The man continued to shout orders and obscenities at those who remained near him, at one point punching one of the clowns in the face who thought it necessary to chime in with their own thoughts.

Judging by the rage that appeared to be present in Shilo's eyes, Olivia concluded that the man who was ordering everyone around was who Shilo was looking for. It was Jug, her brother, and that only confirmed that Shilo was right and that he was still here. That clearly, he was the one in charge and that it was his circus and that by the sounds of it, he was not going anywhere.

Moments later he began to flip out again as Olivia could overhear one of the clowns break to him that several dead bodies had been discovered. He now knew that someone was killing off his men, and when he inquired if anyone had escaped, they brought up the man that Olivia had witnessed get his head crushed, Hayley, and then he said two other girls were seen running around but were nowhere to be found. When he inquired who they were, and the clown mentioned that Shilo was one of them, Jug pulled a knife out and stabbed the clown in the throat, standing over him as the clown dropped to one knee and clutching his neck before slowly laying down and ceasing to move after several seconds passed. Jug then yanked his knife out of the now-dead clown's neck and wiped it on another's sleeve who was standing nearby.

"Find her!" he shouted at the clown who then ran off.

Jug paced back and forth, one clown in a suit with blue hair and the two giants still staying put and awaiting further instruction.

"I don't care if this entire circus goes up in flames. Locate her. If you need to turn over every square inch of this fucking place, do it. I want her fucking head on a platter by night's end. Do you hear me?"

"Yes, sir," the clown and one of the giants said in unison.

The clown and giant who had spoken walked off while one remained by Jug's side, perhaps a bodyguard or awaiting a separate order for himself. A minute later and Jug walked off, headed back towards the big tent with the giant remaining by his side.

Once they were gone, Shilo slowly rose up and looked around. After determining that it was clear, she wasted no time in climbing over the top of the counter and dropping to the ground outside. Olivia quickly followed her, landing beside her and then following as Shilo headed towards the big top as well.

They stayed just off the path, Shilo trying to keep an eye on Jug even though he was too far ahead and almost out of view.

At one point, Shilo carelessly stayed out in the open when the giant following Jug stopped and turned around, but Olivia was quick to pull her out of view and into the shadows before he managed to see her and then reminded Shilo not to get careless now. That they finally had a distraction that was also aiding in wiping out the circus, that they were hot on Jug's trail, and that he only had one person with him.

Olivia tried to think ahead to the fight she knew was

coming and concluded that if she could somehow distract the giant long enough to allow Shilo to slip by unnoticed, Shilo could pursue Jug and take him on by herself and finally put an end to this.

The big top was bigger than expected. As they finally got to the clearing just out in front of it, Shilo and Olivia stayed crouched behind some boxes and watched as Jug entered the tent with the giant.

"Let's sneak around," Shilo whispered, looking around and then pointing off to the right side of where they were.

Shilo led the way, slowly moving behind the boxes and both her and Olivia keeping an eye out for any signs of movement. They didn't want to make a noise and alert Jug or the giant to their presence, but they also didn't want anyone else sneaking up behind them.

As they slowly made their way around the big top, keeping a little bit of a distance from it, the women moved in between a dozen empty tents and unused cages. Shilo and Olivia stopped moving at one point, thinking that they heard someone, but it was only a stiff breeze passing through a nearby tent and causing an old-looking rocking chair to tap up against a dresser with wigs and makeup scattered on top.

After finally reaching the side and then another opening, the big top came into view.

A few noises could be heard coming from inside. The women approached, being sure to look around first before sprinting across the dirt-filled clearing and then entered inside. Once a few feet in, they discovered that there were dozens of cages filled with all kinds of animals, but they weren't alone. The cages weren't just filled with animals. Some of them appeared to have body parts in them too, and upon inspecting the first cage they passed, Shilo and Olivia both became overwhelmed by the stench of rotting flesh.

Both women covered their mouths and noses, gagging, but trying to remain calm and quiet at the same time. Olivia threw up, her vomit passing through her fingers as she began to cough but was able to compose herself quickly. Shilo didn't react the same way and was able to keep herself from vomiting, although she clutched her stomach at one point and had to look away.

Some of the animals in their cages just stared at Shilo and Olivia, not interested or curious by them being there at all. As they continued to pass from cage to cage, they stopped and rushed up to one when they thought they found someone caged up. After getting closer and checking them for a pulse, they realized that they were dead and had been for quite some time.

"Fuck," Shilo whispered in a defeated tone as she stood back up and looked around. "I can't fucking believe this is really happening," she said, a single tear falling down her cheek before she wiped it away.

Olivia put her hand on Shilo's shoulder before they suddenly heard someone talking. They quickly rushed behind one of the nearby animal cages and crawled underneath it as two shadows appeared about a dozen yards away. Some of the animals began to roar and make aggressive noises as the two figures came into view and stood at the center, inspecting the area.

It was Jug and the giant.

Shilo tightened her grip on her knife as Olivia reached over and grabbed her wrist in an attempt to calm her down. Olivia knew Shilo wanted just to rush out and stab him, especially being this close to him, but the moment wasn't right. He wasn't alone. Olivia wasn't sure if he ever would be, but they had to wait and see and couldn't be careless about how they went about their attack.

After the men continued walking around and then entered back into the shadows, their voices soon fading away, Shilo finally let out a sigh that she was holding in and then lowered her head.

Suddenly someone began to shout outside. Shilo and Olivia, at first reluctant to leave their hiding place beneath the animal cage, carefully made their way to the side entrance of the big top and peered outside to see what was going on.

The fire had grown exponentially. It was more than twice the size it was before and had spread so wildly that it was now approaching the big top and there was nothing that anyone was going to be able to do to prevent it.

 # Chapter 22

A multitude of screams raged on outside as the fire barreled its way towards the big top.

Jug could be heard shouting orders at the clowns who retreated and were now trying to protect the biggest tent now, their previous attempts at stopping the fire wasted.

Shilo and Olivia stayed out of sight, returning to the animal area and passing through it, some of the animals snarling at them as they passed. They continued towards the center of the tent where the main show took place, the two large dirt circles surrounded by tall bleachers that lined the entire interior of the central area. Shilo and Olivia stayed close to them, passing through underneath them and keeping an eye on the opening at the front where they could see the shadows of everyone fighting the fire outside.

The top of the tent bowed due to the wind which was certainly aiding the fire in spreading and the gusts carrying smoke inside that stung and made the eyes water.

The women continued until they were on the other

side of the main entertainment area, passing into the other side of the big top which was the opposite side of where the animals were.

Dozens of bodies littered the area. Some were cut up, and limbs were severed and scattered into several small piles including one made up of just heads. Women and men alike, and from the looks of it, several young children as well had been gutted and slaughtered. It looked like a massacre or like it was the end of the world and both Shilo and Olivia were having a hard time comprehending that what they were seeing was real.

Unable to resist it this time, both women vomited as the smell and sight of the horrors in front of them were too much to bear. They gagged and coughed uncontrollably, running out of the area and back out into the center of the big top, collapsing by each other's side in one of the dirt-filled rings and retching while keeled over.

Suddenly someone shouted.

Shilo and Olivia, still shaken and sick to their stomachs quickly looked over and saw one of the clowns standing on the inside of the tent. He was staring directly at them and was pointing to them before turning and shouting at the others still fighting the fire just outside.

The two women began to run to the other side of the tent where the animals were as several of the other clowns, Jug, and the two giants entered quickly giving pursuit.

"Run!" Shilo screamed as she and Olivia, already running as fast as they could, continued through the bleachers as the clowns quickly approached and shortened the distance between them.

Shilo and Olivia were soon back where the animals were. With their sudden appearance, several of the animals became startled and started to move wildly in their cages as the clowns shouting was quickly approaching.

"I have an idea!" Shilo shouted as she ran up to one of the cages, one containing two intimidating-looking hyenas.

Shilo hesitated and took a deep breath as she lifted a lever on the side of the cage and the gate suddenly unlocked.

Olivia knew exactly what Shilo was up to and quickly got out of the way. Just as she did, two clowns quickly entered the area and Shilo flung the cage open, the hyenas quickly rushing out and pouncing towards the clowns.

The clowns began to scream in pain as the hyenas latched onto them, one biting into the side of one's neck while the other chomped down on the other's arm and began to shake him violently.

Shilo and Olivia then quickly moved cage to cage, opening each one as the hyenas continued to maul the clowns while more of them, including the giants, entered the area.

One of the giants kicked one of the hyenas, the one clown it was on obviously dead. The other giant grabbed the other hyena and lifted it into the air, strangling it with his mighty hands while the clown it had been on clutched his arm in horror. His lower arm was barely still attached at the elbow and dangled, blood rushing out of a severed artery.

Dozens of animals now poured out of their cages and rushed either towards the clowns or ran out of the tent to escape. From an alligator that slid out and disappeared into the shadows beneath its cage, to a lion that tackled one of the giants and began to chomp down on his head, Jug's men were now quickly being dispatched.

The odds were now quickly beginning to lean in Shilo and Olivia's favor even though now they were stuck in the midst of pure chaos as the scene around them unfolded.

In the middle of everything going on Olivia felt someone grab her arm. She panicked, and as she turned, she went to swing her knife but stopped mid-swing when she realized it was Shilo. Shilo pulled Olivia in the direction of the exit, both then rushing out into the open only to quickly stop once they got outside.

In front of them and now staring them down was a bear.

At some point in the chaos of the animals being released, one of the women had released a bear and it rushed outside with some of the other animals who were now no longer in sight. Only the bear stayed close to the tent and was now slowly walking directly at the women.

Shilo and Olivia began to back up as the bear quickly stood up on its hind legs, letting out a ferocious roar as saliva launched from its jaws and flew through the air.

"What the fuck do we do?" Olivia shouted as Shilo and her stumbled while still moving back.

Suddenly one of the giants came walking out of the tent with a large steel pipe in his hand. He looked over at the women and began to approach them, completely ignoring the bear and only glancing over at it once it started to charge forward.

He swung his pipe at it, striking the bear in the side of the head but it wasn't enough to make it stop crashing into him. The giant tried to resist being knocked over, but the bear was easily too strong for him and rolled on top of him, starting to swat its massive claws at his face while randomly snapping its jaws down at him.

Two clowns came out of the tent and tried to help the giant, swinging bats, and stabbing at the bear with knives but the bear knocked both of them down with a single swing. They were successful in redirecting the bear's attention, however, and this gave the bloodied giant enough time to get to his feet. He then approached the bear who glanced back and snarled at him, swinging one of its paws around but missing him. The clowns then moved in and landed a few blows on the bear before the bear's attention turned to them and then the giant would attack.

The bear was outnumbered.

While terrified of it, Shilo and Olivia were both praying the bear could help them by taking out a few more of Jug's men.

Suddenly a hyena came rushing out of the tent and ran right into one of the clowns, knocking him forward towards the bear. He looked up and let out a scream as the bear chomped down on his head and his body went limp.

Now it was just the giant and one other clown.

A few seconds later and Jug appeared, stepping out of the tent and quickly spotting the women taking cover by some boxes.

A smile crossed his face when he made eye contact with Shilo, and that was when Olivia grabbed Shilo's arm and began to run in the opposite direction.

As they ran around towards the front of the tent, the fire now burning structures just a dozen yards away and the air filled with ash and embers raining down, a clown in a suit with blue hair quickly stepped into view and caused the women to come to a stop. He flipped a butterfly knife around in his hand while he started to laugh, brushing his hair to the side with his other hand before beginning to walk towards them.

The women prepared themselves, glancing behind them to make sure no one else was approaching from the rear before returning their attention to the clown.

As he got closer, the women could tell that his face had been singed by the fire. Black soot was covering parts of what was once a face covered in all white and blue makeup.

He lunged forward with his knife in an attempt to go for Shilo first as she jumped out of the way. He then turned and tried to stab Olivia, his knife running along the side of her arm and cutting through her flesh with ease.

Olivia let out a shout as blood began to flow from the wound.

Shilo then lunged at the clown, her knife colliding with his back but the blade hitting something hard which Olivia could only assume was his shoulder blade.

He grunted in pain as he tried to reach over his shoulder and pull the knife out, turning around and facing Shilo who was now weaponless. He screamed at her, raising his arm with his knife in hand. Olivia then rushed forward, thrusting her knife into the clown's side. Shilo jumped at the clown then, reaching up and grabbing his hand and pulling his knife from it while his attention was on Olivia's knife in his side, and then Shilo took his knife and slashed his throat in a single motion. Olivia maintained her grip on her knife, the blade sliding out of the clown's side as he fell to the ground and began to gurgle and drown in his blood.

Suddenly there was movement from the side. Shilo and Olivia looked over and saw a bloodied and severely injured bear approaching and carrying someone's severed arm in its mouth. As the bear approached, it dropped the arm and stood up again, letting out another roar before lowering and charging towards the women.

"Run!" Olivia yelled, but before they could even begin to get away, the bear was already crashing into them and sending them to the ground.

The bear had charged right through them but continued running. It could have turned and begun to attack, but instead, it ignored the women. When Shilo and Olivia looked up at it, it turned and tried to run down the path that led up to the big tent, but the fire quickly jumped across and surrounded the bear, causing it to roar and cry in pain as its fur caught on fire.

Seconds later the bear turned and began to run towards the women again. The only difference this time was that the bear was on fire.

Shilo and Olivia quickly got to their feet and ran for the front entrance of the tent, turning and entering inside as the bear crashed into a tent nearby causing it to collapse and burst into flames. Ignited fabric flew throughout the air and landed near the entrance and caused the fire to finally begin its consumption of the big top.

The way out of the front was now blocked as the fire quickly shot up, traveling straight up as it began to make its way in both directions as the two women slowly backed up towards the center and watched in horror.

"There you are," a voice said behind the women.

Olivia turned around, but as she did, she felt something sharp pierce her side. When she looked down, she saw a hand holding onto a small knife now in her side. When she looked up, she was now staring into Jug's eyes who was focused entirely on his sister.

"If you'll excuse me, my sister and I have some unfinished family business to attend to," he said as he pulled the knife out and pushed Olivia away, causing her to fall to the ground as she clutched her side in pain.

"Olivia!" Shilo shouted as Jug suddenly lunged at her with his knife.

Shilo quickly stepped to the side, causing Jug to miss, and then rushed over to Olivia as Jug slowly turned around and watched her arrive at Olivia's side.

"Keep the pressure on it!" she informed after taking a quick look at her wound.

"Behind you!" Olivia warned as Jug lunged at Shilo, but she got out of the way just in time.

Olivia stuck her leg out and caused Jug to stumble forward into the wood that encircled the dirt-filled ring. He then fell to his knees on the other side, his top hat flying off his head and rolling away.

Letting out a rage-filled yell he stood back up and took his jacket off and threw it aside, revealing arms covered in tattoos. He pulled on his suspenders while beginning to walk around the wood that circled the area. His focus was solely on Shilo as Olivia crawled over the wood and began to back away at Shilo's direction. She wanted to face her brother alone, and while Olivia knew that fighting together would be better and give them the advantage, she was far too injured and in no condition to try and fight.

"You fucking ruined everything," Jug said to Shilo, faking a lunge at her and trying to intimidate Shilo with his knife.

"You're sick. What you're doing here, what you've done. All those people? How could you do such things?" Shilo asked, trying to keep the center beam of the tent in between her and her brother.

"I could lie and say I never meant for any of this to happen, but the truth is, I did," he said, stepping over the wood and now standing in the ring.

Shilo jumped to the other side of the beam as Jug charged forward, his knife slashing across the wood and narrowly missing Shilo. She turned and tried to slash her knife at Jug, slightly grazing his arm and cutting through his skin in the process.

He let out a laugh after examining the wound, licking the small trail of blood that came from it before leaning back and letting out a loud cackle.

"Oh, I'm going to have so much fun skinning and killing you Shilo. This is going to be so enjoyable for me."

"You can try," Shilo replied, suddenly lunging at her brother and catching him off guard.

Shilo slashed at him wildly several times as he

continued to step back, suddenly sidestepping and quickly slashing his knife at Shilo's face. She screamed and immediately put her hand on her face, turning around and stumbling to one knee.

"Shilo!" Olivia yelled as she watched in horror.

Jug let out a laugh as he walked a few feet in the opposite direction of Shilo, looking up as the fire was now reaching the top of the tent and pieces of fabric began to fall from above.

Olivia looked back over to Shilo who was holding her hand that was covered in blood. She glanced over to Olivia, and that was when she realized that Shilo was not actually hurt that bad. Jug's knife must have just barely cut her, but it was enough to cause her to bleed. She was making it seem like she was injured worse than she was, and as Jug began to approach her from behind, Shilo suddenly turned and stabbed him in the thigh.

Jug let out a scream as he stumbled back and fell into the center beam, Shilo's knife protruding from the center of his leg.

Shilo began to punch him in the face several times until he managed to grab her and throw her backward. She fell onto her back as Jug yanked the knife out of his leg, the blood oozing out in between his fingers as he tried to apply pressure to the wound.

He then proceeded to scream as he quickly limped towards Shilo, throwing himself on top of her and struggling to try and get his hands on her throat. They rolled around several times, with Jug slamming her head into the ground several times until Shilo kneed him in the groin. As he stood up, Shilo got up and jumped on his back, wrapping her arms around him and squeezing him as tight as she could. He tried to shake her free but to no avail. At one point Shilo bit down on one of Jug's ears and turned her head sharply, ripping a large chunk off and then spitting it aside as Jug reached up and managed to grab onto her hair. He tried desperately to pull her off, but he couldn't, so he threw himself back into the beam with such force that the beam actually shook in place and caused the ceiling of the tent to begin to buckle. Shilo took the brunt of the hit into the beam which caused her to yell and loosen her grip on him and fall to the ground.

Jug, clutching the side of his head with one of his hands and trying to catch his breath slowly turned around. As he did, and Shilo who was still on the ground looked over, both of their eyes locked onto Jug's knife sticking out of the dirt at the same time. Without hesitation the both of them lunged for it, reaching it at the same time and causing dirt to fly up into the air as a large piece of a wooden beam from above crashed through the bleachers on the far side of the center of the tent.

Shilo, Jug, and Olivia all looked up as the top of the tent began to come down now. Bits and pieces of the beams holding the top up began to fall with large chunks of burning cloth raining down.

Olivia then looked back to the two fighting siblings

as Shilo managed to find the knife beneath the dirt and she thrust the knife up into Jug's stomach. He grabbed onto her hands and let out a yell as the center beam beside them suddenly tilted and began to lean in their direction.

"Watch out!" Olivia shouted, covering her face as the wood let out a loud snap and came crashing down, sending dirt, debris, and flaming cloth throughout the air.

Olivia opened her eyes several seconds later and quickly looked up, the fire now scattered around and the entire big top coming down all around them. That was when she saw Shilo sitting beside the wooden beam, but Jug was nowhere in sight. Olivia then fought her hardest to get to her feet, moving in between pieces of fallen beams, burning fabric, and large flames to try and get to Shilo who was looking around at the apocalyptic sight around them.

"Shilo!" Olivia shouted as she fell forward beside her, noticing two legs to her left underneath the large center beam.

"Are you okay?" Olivia asked as Shilo looked dazed and confused, blood still coming from the small gash across the side of the top of her head.

Shilo nodded silently, slowly getting up with the knife she had stabbed Jug in the stomach with just moments before. Shilo walked around the fallen beam, and Olivia followed, watching as Shilo knelt over her brother who appeared to still be alive but had his entire lower body from the waist down trapped beneath the beam.

Jug coughed several times, blood now coming out of his mouth and flowing in a single stream down the side of his face. He looked over at Shilo who looked down at him, knife still in hand.

"My only regret," he said with a cough. "Was not being able to watch you die."

Shilo then thrust Jug's own knife into his chest. He reached up and grabbed onto her hair with one hand and wrapped his other hand around her throat, squeezing it with whatever strength he had left that he could muster.

The two siblings stared into each other's eyes, one trying to outlast the other as Shilo pushed the knife further and further into his chest and twisted it, causing him to cough up more blood. A few seconds later and Jug let out a long exhale as his arms slowly released Shilo and lowered until they were at his side.

Shilo stared at her brother for a few seconds before turning back to Olivia, tears both in her eyes and flowing down her cheeks.

"That's it," Shilo said. "It's all over."

"I witnessed the end myself," Olivia responded, looking around at the flames.

Shilo then quickly got up and put herself under Oliva's shoulder, lifting her and beginning to walk towards a tear in the rear of the tent, dodging jumping flames and pieces of fabric that were somehow still falling from above. Once they reached the opening and exited the tent, Shilo continued to aid Olivia, not stopping until they circled around and got to the metal fence that surrounded the circus. They were now far enough from the fire that they could breathe again and began to cough as they fought for air.

The two women sat beside the fence far enough from anything that could catch on fire and no longer in any danger from the flames. They watched as whatever was left of the big top that had not collapsed while they were inside, finally fell and lit on fire too.

"Do you hear that?" Olivia asked, still clutching her side with one hand but now pointing off in the direction of where the gate that Emma had escaped through was.

Shilo listened for a moment before she nodded.

It was sirens and a lot of them.

"C'mon," Shilo said, helping Olivia get up again and then beginning to walk along the fence in the direction of the gate. "Let's finally get out of here."

Suddenly a figure appeared within the smoke.

Shilo and Olivia froze and stared in horror as the figure began to walk towards them, revealing the old woman who they had completely forgotten. She approached slowly, stopping a few dozen yards away from the two women.

"I warned him you would be the end of all of this," she said, raising one hand and pointing her finger at Shilo. "He didn't want to listen to me. His arrogance was his downfall."

Shilo began to walk with Olivia back towards the center path, all the tents nearby nothing but smoldering piles of ash now. The old lady followed, slowly, before suddenly revealing a large knife in her hand and charging after Shilo and Olivia.

Shilo picked up the pace, Olivia trying to help as much as she could as shouting could be heard quickly approached.

"Get down!" someone yelled, and Shilo and Olivia both fell forward into the dirt.

Several gunshots suddenly rang out.

Shilo and Olivia covered their heads until the gunfire stopped and then glanced up, a young cop standing a dozen yards away with his weapon raised and pointed at the old woman behind them. When they looked back to her, she was clutching her chest, and after a few seconds, dropped the knife and fell over, gasping for breath before finally falling into silence.

"Are the two of you okay?" the cop asked, looking at them in horror while still keeping his gun pointed towards the old woman.

That was when Shilo and Olivia noticed a familiar face stepping out of one of the dozen cop cars that had pulled up with several fire trucks and a few ambulances right behind them.

It was Emma.

Shilo and Olivia both sighed in relief as Shilo helped Olivia up again.

"Now we can finally get out of here," Shilo joked.

"Together," Olivia added, both women glancing over at each other and sharing a smile as they headed in the direction of the ambulances, Emma and several paramedics running towards them while firefighters and cops rushed into the area, flashing red and blue lights illuminating the smoke-filled sky.

Acknowledgements

I would like to give thanks to my wife and parents for their unwavering support.

I would also like to thank my fans, give a special shout out to Mercedes, and to those who have supported me, read my work, or just given suggestions and cheered me on.

I would not have reached this point without you.

Author Bio

William Joseph was born in Lakewood New Jersey. He grew up in nearby Pine Beach New Jersey and now resides in Barnegat, NJ. An only child and highly imaginative, William Joseph spent a lot of time writing growing up, but it wasn't until he finally felt that he had a story to tell with THIS IS WAR that he stuck with it from beginning to end. During this time, William Joseph attended Ocean County College and graduated with honors and two degrees. While in college, he also attended a creative writing class, where, for the first time he shared his work with other people. Sharing a short story with them and seeing how he could emotionally connect with his readers got him hooked. His short story was published in his college's literary magazine, and since then, the pursuit for publishing his work began, as well as the dedication and dream of writing more books and stories to share with the world.

Social Media Addresses:

Facebook: @authorwilliamjoseph
Instagram: @authorwilliamj
Twitter: @authorwilliamj

Website: authorwilliamjoseph.weebly.com

Made in the USA
Coppell, TX
04 November 2022

85765756R00134